God,

the Moon,

and Other

Megafauna

THE RICHARD SULLIVAN PRIZE IN SHORT FICTION

Editors
William O'Rourke and Valerie Sayers

God,
the Moon,
and Other
Megafauna

Stories by

KELLIE WELLS

University of Notre Dame Press

Notre Dame, Indiana

Published by the University of Notre Dame Press
Notre Dame, Indiana 46556
undpress.nd.edu
All Rights Reserved

Library of Congress Cataloging-in-Publication Data

Names: Wells, Kellie, 1962– author.
Title: God, the moon, and other megafauna : stories / by Kellie Wells.
Description: Notre Dame, Indiana : University of Notre Dame Press, [2017] |
    Series: The Richard Sullivan Prize in Short Fiction |
Identifiers: LCCN 2017025413 (print) | LCCN 2017025444 (ebook) | ISBN
    9780268102272 (pdf) | ISBN 9780268102289 (epub) | ISBN 9780268102258
    (hardback) | ISBN 0268102252 (hardcover) | ISBN 9780268102265 (paper)
Subjects: | BISAC: FICTION / Short Stories (single author). | LITERARY
    CRITICISM / Short Stories. | FICTION / General.
Classification: LCC PS3623.E47 (ebook) | LCC PS3623.E47 A6 2017 (print) | DDC
    813/.6—dc23
LC record available at https://lccn.loc.gov/2017025413

∞*This paper meets the requirements of ANSI/NISO Z39.48-1992
(Permanence of Paper).*

CONTENTS

FAUNA

APOCALYPSE

ACKNOWLEDGMENTS

These stories have appeared previously in literary journals: "A Unified Theory of Human Behavior," in *American Short Fiction*; "L'Enfant du Paradis," in *Unstuck*; "Moon, Moon, My Honey," in the *Kenyon Review*; "Threnody," in *Ninth Letter*; "In the Hatred of a Minute," in *Nimrod*; "Ever After," in *Fairy Tale Review*; "Telling the Chicken," in *CutBank*; "Kansas," in *Transmission*; "The Rising Girl," in the *Kenyon Review;* "Animalmancy," in the *Normal School*; "The Girl, the Wolf, the Crone," in *Fairy Tale Review* and in the anthology *My Mother She Killed Me, My Father He Ate Me: Forty New Fairy Tales* (Penguin); "The Grift of the Magpie," in *Western Humanities Review*; "The Incinerating Place," in *Puerto del Sol*; "The Sorrows," in *Ninth Letter*; "The Arse End of the World" in *Fairy Tale Review*.

Thank you to Adeena Reitberger, Matt Williamson, David Lynn, Sergei Lobanov-Rostovsky, Jodee Stanley, Kate Bernheimer, Janice Kidd, Zoey Larsen, Michael Mejia, and Randa Jarrar, for their editorial advice and encouragement; Rick Krizman, for having a sharp eye; and Tom Mahoney, for his unwavering enthusiasm, love, and shameless paronomasia. Also a shout-out to fairy tales, dogs, and crones, without which my life would be wanting and my imagination beggared.

MOON

In the Beginning

There was so much absence.

A Unified Theory of
Human Behavior

The girl hadn't meant to break her arm, not completely. She'd thought just a hairline fracture, something borderline enough to warrant a cast. People would be compelled to sign the cast with short jokes and well wishes and the sorts of generic slogans reserved for yearbooks. She liked scripted interactions, and the thought of classmates signing their names to her was also appealing, as though she were a love letter, a confession, a suicide note, a pact with the devil. Perhaps she'd practice the signatures and then sign others' names to harmless agreements, homeroom monitor for the month of February, say, the 4:00 p.m. Tuesday slot for glee club tryouts. People would say, *Jeremy Webster? Dude couldn't carry a tune if it was packed in a suitcase*, and they'd snicker at the thought of this boy with his mouth rounded uncertainly in song standing next to Gregory Markovich, a thin boy, voice sweet as a violin, who sang so well he'd been getting shoved into lockers and fat kids for as long as she could remember.

She'd once written a note to her father in her mother's yearning script, and her father still kept it inside the dresser drawer with handkerchiefs and tie clips and golf tees. She was a capable forger.

The pins in her arm were painful, but she liked the thought of being pulled aside at airports, suspected of complicated criminality by embittered security guards. Her father had told her that gruff handling by security was misdirected, compensation for a paltry paycheck. He'd tried once to encourage the sullen person waving the metal-detecting wand along his torso to smile defiantly even when the world seemed hostile toward his ambitions. Her father was a motivational speaker, and he frequently traveled to cities with palm trees, cities where people wore short sleeves in February.

She'd once read about young girls who swallowed balloons full of drugs, which was a method of smuggling that defied detection so long as the drugs didn't leak from the pouch and cause the girls to foam at the mouth and seize, and she thought about things she could swallow and keep secret from the people around her. She liked swallowing, as a rule, liked feeling things carried along inside her by a reliable mechanism, though if she thought about it with too much particularity, the idea would make her throat constrict and she'd have to suck a wedge of lemon to antidote it. Perhaps she'd eat the heavily inked declarations of love she sometimes found crumpled in the trash can of the study hall, or the glass eye she once found at the bottom of the Victory Hills swimming pool. The words would likely dissolve in stomach acid, but the brown eye would sit inside her, secretly observing people who would not suspect she had an eye in her stomach. She thought the kids who liked to read science fiction might be able to imagine such a thing if she gave them clues. They were fanciful, in a predictable way, and mostly good natured, wearing T-shirts and ragged trousers and washing their hair only once a week, if that, and sometimes they made her heart clutch because she knew they trusted that the universe was basically just, or would become so once they reached adulthood. To them this meant that one day the popular boys would grow up to be life insurance salesmen, would suffer from the most intractable form of seborrheic dermatitis, become addicted to painkillers after motorcycle accidents, and have a series of loveless affairs in mildewed hotel rooms while their wives bought twelve packs of things they didn't need at the Dollar General and compulsively scrapbooked. There were so many things the girl knew she'd never be suspected of, and this made her think of her dog, who twitched and emitted stifled barks as he slept curled in the sunlight that pooled on her bed. It looked to her as though the dog had been beamed there from a faraway cosmos, so perfectly did he fit inside the circle of light, and he was transmitting information he'd collected throughout the day back to his home planet, which was a cheerful place where squirrels fell steadily from trees like leaves in autumn. It was a place the dog missed keenly, though he was dutiful and committed to his mission, and she could see this in his eyes when he rested his head on her foot.

Just before the girl fell from the tree, she thought about her English teacher, Mrs. Stashwick, who wore orange lipstick, had a Himalayan Siamese cat named Sherpa, made recently thin by chemo, and whose favorite poem featured a woman whose death had been interrupted by the buzzing of a fly. The girl felt it was a little unprofessional of a soon-to-be corpse to be noticing flies in its final seconds rather than thumbing through a mental photo album of its life, but she didn't mention this to Mrs. Stashwick, whose nose ran chronically. The girl made a note in the margin, however, for she wished to know the correct protocol for any situation that might arise. Eric Cotsonas, who frequently sat next to her, believed himself to be a comic genius, and always eyeballed her notes like a raptor tracking a vole, leaned over and whispered, *Yeah, flies seem like the last thing that should be on a dead person's mind*, then he laughed through his nose, and Mrs. Stashwick glared at him with such palpable scorn he began to swallow audibly.

After the fly poem, Mrs. Stashwick talked about abstraction and then she asked the class to define love. "If love were an animal," said Mrs. Stashwick, "what animal would it be? If love were a breakfast food . . . if love were a musical instrument . . ." Teachers were always making assignments like this. The girl admired the teachers' thick-skinned resolve when it came to ignoring, in such moments, the snorting derision of the students. That night, at home, the girl stared at the assignment until she got the hiccups, and then she drank a glass of water upside down. Back at her desk, she wrote, *Love is an extinction that eats the fertilized eggs of ostriches and plays accordion with its gnarled feet.* She got up, looked in the mirror, colored her lips blue with her pen, and pressed them to the page. People were always going on and on about love, as if anyone knew the first thing about it. She thought it was like teleportation, something that might happen in the future if the right scientists were given high-quality equipment and free rein to be a little diabolical, something that would likely dismember the bodies of the first few volunteers.

The girl's mother was no longer alive, but if she had been, she would have forbidden the girl from climbing a tree ever again. She might even have given the offending tree a good whack in its trunk with an axe, just to let the tree know the girl would not be nature's idle patsy, not if she could help it. The girl's father said one nasty spill needn't put an end to her climbing days forever—*get back up on that horse!*—and then he whinnied and laughed and cuffed the girl on the good shoulder, told her she was a valuable human being, with or without the use of her arm. Her father frequently mixed metaphors or used improbable analogies, and he suffered from insomnia. The girl tried to imagine the shape of the permanent crook the doctor said she'd now have in her forearm, her body the victim of a new geometry. Sometimes she found herself wishing her father would slip into the river and never resurface. Later, on a spring morning, a person jogging along the path that flanked the river might hear ghostly encouragements bubble up through the water, and when the jogger got home and soaped off the sweat in the shower, he'd feel a good deal better about himself, and this feeling would be further confirmed by the kind of vital and effortless day he would have, but forever after he would try, fruitlessly, to recapture what he thought was the endorphin-induced buoyancy of that day, and eventually he would have to have knee replacements, the first one at the age of forty-five. The girl thought she, too, would like to have her knees replaced, though with what she wasn't certain. Ornamental cabbages perhaps, small television sets, the skulls of famous animals, something that would make her the focus of a tabloid talk show. She thought her life might be more interesting if she lived it in such a way as to cause people to hurl accusations at her.

Her mother's death had been the best thing that ever happened to her father, who had spent most nights in a well-worn club chair in his den, falling asleep, when he was able, with a half-empty tumbler of scotch in his hands, the ice melting and causing the amber liquid to grow pale by morning. The girl sometimes awoke late at night, stole downstairs, and laid a hand on her father's belly, watched

it rise and fall. The diluted sunsets of winter alwa
of her father.

There was an accident and when her father
driving the girl home from volleyball practice. The ac
far from the school, and he swung the car around in the middle of
the street, like the cops do on television when the dispatcher tells
them there's a robbery in progress in a neighborhood nearby, and
when the girl and her father arrived at the scene, there were police
cars and an ambulance and a fire engine blocking the road. The lights
reminded her of the roller-skating rink, and she fingered the blister
on the back of her heel.

Her father left the car running in the middle of the street, left
the door open, and walked into the variously uniformed people, two
of whom seized his shoulders and prevented him from passing. The
girl also got out of the car, but she closed the door, and she went instead to the side of the road, where she began to pick up pieces of
glass that made her think of the shaved ice she'd had the previous
weekend at the carnival. She put the glass in her pocket.

Later she would place the bits of glass on her dresser. When she
looked at them, her mouth would grow cold, as though she were
sucking on ice, and she'd think about how beautifully things can
break. Eventually, she would deposit the shards in her mother's
shoes, in the toes. Later yet, she would come home to find her
mother's clothing, including the shoes, gone, and she would ask her
father what had happened to her mother's belongings. The girl
would feel bad when she thought of a woman on a tight budget slipping her foot into a pump and pricking her toe on a fragment of
glass, the woman thinking at first she'd been bitten. Her foot would
fly out of the shoe, like a fairy tale in reverse. What if, wondered the
girl, the tale were actually about a woman who marries a doting
prince but longs for a life of drudgery and ill treatment, a woman
who hates wearing shoes altogether? Eden Reynolds, the girl's
locker mate at school, had swapped a boyfriend who left peanut
M&M's inside her binder for one who bruised her wrist when he
pulled her out of a conversation. This sort of thing happened all the
time for Pete's sake, and who was to say Eden Reynolds was better

off with the M&M's? The girl, who had kissed one boy experimentally, felt she was not seasoned enough in romantic entanglements to make such a judgment. She also thought happy people were a little suspicious, in that they tended to get winded more easily and were frequently drawn to people with bad skin, just something she'd observed. She kept such observations in a notebook and referred to them periodically. She felt she was on the verge of a unified theory of human behavior. She also thought if this theory fell into the wrong hands, it could be real trouble, so she sometimes tore pages out of the notebook and hid them beneath flowerpots and jars of nails and dusty kitchen appliances. She'd hidden one in her mother's pocketbook, the one her mother had had with her in the car. Fortunately, that page the girl had committed to memory. It was so essential to her theory, she felt it was a danger even to think about it much, lest she mumble it in her sleep, so she tried to think only in a redacted manner: *Girls who* ▬▬▬▬▬▬▬ *congenital sorrow.* ▬▬▬▬▬▬ *famished babies* ▬▬▬▬ *unhygienic* ▬▬▬ *river rocks. Singing* ▬▬▬▬▬ *until they die.*

At the accident site, she overheard a police officer telling an EMT that they'd found an arm many feet away from the car and that it was a beautiful arm, unharmed save for the severing, with a delicate wrist still wearing an expensive bracelet. Her mother had wrists that called to mind a mythical bird, so long and fine they seemed to the girl supernatural, like something that would one day become a relic people believed could cure arthritis or cause crops to flourish. Later, the girl thought about it and realized, however, this could not have been her mother's arm, because her mother rarely wore bracelets, never wore a watch. They slid from her hands onto the floor, and this had made her mother angry. Her mother had a list in a drawer of all the things she'd lost, and she showed it once to the girl. At the bottom of the list, she'd penned *my figure, my mind, my will to live, ha!* Even rings had to be specially sized, as they seemed never to be small enough, always sliding from the reeds of her mother's fingers into the dishwater. With this realization came a secondary realization, which was that other people had likely died in the automobile accident, and she thought the world, which she knew was a notoriously unreliable place (the girl was nobody's dupe) could be quite ruthless in its deceptions, the sort of place where many children, at the same moment, envisioned the severed limbs of their parents, only to realize later that they belonged to someone else. Realizations, thought the girl, though sometimes helpful, did so little to change an outcome. At this moment, the girl deeply resented the absence of both logic and magic in the world.

During the funeral service, the girl's mother sat inside an urn, charred particles settling. It was a handsome vessel, made of polished pebble stone, intricately veined, and was stationed in front of a framed photograph. The girl thought about dust gathering on the outside of the urn, perhaps envious of the class of dust that dwelled inside, and she imagined one day the peasant dust would storm the palace, demand to be allowed entrance, and likely oust the dust of her mother, and it would start all over again until the urn itself crumbled to dust, and this was the history of the world, as well as the story of a future any rookie soothsayer could safely predict. This was as it must be, she supposed, but having to sit in front of this smiling photograph of her mother as she gazed out benevolently at the mourners, her face young and brightly masked with cosmetics, this the girl found appalling. Her mother would not wish to be remembered smiling affably nor amidst flowers.

At home, in the living room, sitting on the sofa with a sweating glass in hand, the girl's father told her that the mother had, in her will, asked that her ashes be scattered in the river, and before she could think better of it, the girl expelled a forceful snort. It was just like her mother to make a joke, even now. The river, that was a good one. Her mother had hated all bodies of water, not least of all her own. When the girl informed her mother that the brain was 85% water, a miscellaneous look crossed her mother's face, and she clutched her daughter's arm and said, "What a terrible thing to say."

The girl considered the word *will* and remembered what her mother had written at the bottom of her list of lost things. Wasn't a will precisely what a person no longer had when she stopped breathing? If her mother had had a will, had had any say in the matter, she would surely have vetoed that ridiculous photograph. Her father's sleepless face looked ancient at that moment, of a biblical age, and she decided to try to cheer him up a little, so she told him the story they'd discussed in social studies last year, in their space exploration unit, about the astrogeologist who had schooled the astronauts in the moon's surface before they traveled there. He knew everything it was possible to know about it from a distance, and he was so thoroughly smitten with this exotic but reachable destination that he requested a burial amidst the craters when he died, and he's now the only person to be in permanent residence on the moon. The girl had at first misunderstood and thought one of the moon missions had scattered the man's remains there, and so she asked the teacher whether or not the man's ashes had ever actually landed on the surface of the moon or just drifted in the atmosphere. She pictured his ashes floating like excess food in a fish tank, drifting above but never settling onto the surface, so close to where he longed to be but too finespun to land, too weightless to make an impression, the cremated body lacking the necessary anchoring heft to moor itself on the moon's fickle surface. The teacher explained that a lipstick-sized tube of the crumbled dust of the man was carried to the moon by a probe, which crashed into the ground. He told the class that, because there's no wind on the moon, all footprints remain there forever. The girl thought a man floating inside an empty tube of lipstick alone on the moon, settled perhaps in the heel of an eternal footprint, was about as sad a story as she'd ever heard, and she wondered now why in the world she'd thought her father might find it encouraging. She touched her father's hand, which looked young and well rested and alien, as though it were on loan from another body, then she went to the kitchen to get more ice.

The girl's father began to drink more after the funeral, which meant there would be no scotch left in the glass or in the bottle come morning. The father now took medication for sleep, and the girl put her ear to her father's murmuring lips, hoping they'd tell her something she'd like to know, for example whether the human heart, which weighs between eight and ten ounces, becomes lighter or heavier when it feels love, but the sound his lips made was like water trickling from a faucet. Heavier, thought the girl, surely. Sometimes, after a long night of dreaming, the girl lay as still as she could on her bed and pretended she was being prepped for exploratory surgery. She did not wish to recollect her dreams, which made her chest feel heavy, as though someone had planted a shot put atop her sternum as she slept. It took great effort for her to lift herself from the bed. As she listened to the burbling sound that came from her father's mouth, she imagined he prayed that the heart of the world would stop beating. Her father's heart had an irregularity that necessitated a course of antibiotics any time he got his teeth cleaned, and she worried that in between dental visits a vigorous brushing might dislodge bacteria that would stop his heart cold, like a hand on a metronome. Sometimes she saw her father clean his teeth with unseemly gusto.

The girl discovered she could go a whole day without drinking. She tried this out after watching a television show about a man in India who had for years been able to slake his modest thirst with his own saliva. There were round-the-clock witnesses who swore his days were free of refreshment. The girl thought the thirstless man's loose, disheveled skin did have a vague appearance of mummification about it. She thought having a body that never needed a drink could solve a lot of problems, especially if your plane crash landed in the middle of the desert. Most people who found themselves unexpectedly in the desert seemed not to possess this gift, however, and they were forced to subsist on the finest droplets of moisture and the limbs of fallen comrades. What *National Geographic* made clear was that the world was always demanding a person make preposterous choices, albeit in beautiful places. If the girl had to choose between being fatally parched and, say, being ravaged by sand fleas as she trudged around in search of water, she was certain she'd try her luck with her own saliva. The girl's mother once told her that the thing she was most proud of was not being able to swim, and the girl did think her mother had looked a little smug whenever she stood behind the sliding glass door and watched her daughter corkscrew down the slide at a hotel swimming pool.

Eventually there would come a moment when the girl's father would stop drinking and begin taking courses at night at the community college, but before this, long before becoming a motivational speaker, before the accident, when her father still sometimes wore pajamas and flossed his teeth and slept in a bed, he worked as an accountant and did the books for a business that sold airplane parts. In the course of his work, he met a German mechanic who told him, confidentially, that soon the planes of a particular American airline would begin to fall from the sky in great numbers, because this airline was a bottom-line skinflint when it came to maintenance, and the cheap, refurbished parts these planes were held together with would soon begin to fail en masse. Her mother had loved the music of Buddy Holly, who died in a plane crash, and at night she could be heard stepping rhythmically upstairs in her bedroom as the music slipped beneath the door, which caused the girl's father to draw his daughter to him and rest his chin on her head. When she smelled the acetone smell that wafted to her from her father's glass, she thought of her mother removing the color from her toenails. She left behind tissues mottled with red smears. The girl had never seen her mother bleed, and the thought of blood coursing eagerly beneath her skin, just waiting to break the surface, both terrified and reassured her. Those toes were one of the most surprising things about the girl's mother, who dressed in pastels and looked like the farthest edge of a watercolor painting, where all color surrenders to its absence. The girl loved her mother's feet disproportionately. Until the accident made it needless to do so, the girl thought every day of her mother's death, imagined her falling from a high building with a crenellated rooftop, the mother's body and spirit both leaden and reconciled to gravity, like a sack of flour thrown from a truck. Once she dreamt that she held all her mother's blood cupped in her hands while her mother waited for it in a small, unfurnished room far away, and, if the girl didn't pour it into a bottle and deliver it to her mother in time, it would mean that her mother had never existed. It would mean *she* had never existed, had never gone to school or eaten tacos or had a dog, things she quite liked, would mean she'd never had this dream. Ultimately, it would mean there was no such thing as love. With every step she took toward it, the room receded. After her mother died, the girl saw herself rising into the air quickly toward the top of that same building, and the thought sometimes made her scream involuntarily during algebra. The pitying look this provoked in the teacher made her want to quietly jab a pencil into her own eye.

So the mother died and the father sobered up and pursued a new career path, which the girl could not help but think was a terrible betrayal, not that he might be happy while his wife could no longer even drink a glass of water, but that he had the gall to motivate other people whose wives had yet to die tragically, whose children had never looked at their arms with such distant scorn that they pitched themselves from trees. That was just inconsiderate, and she thought about publishing an open letter in the newspaper, addressed to the people he motivated. She imagined they, too, would stop drinking, and the thought made her stomach feel like a balled fist. The girl could think of few things worse than a grown man asking a child for forgiveness. Those twelve steps never stopped to consider how objectionable contrition can be for the people whose lives had been built upon the need of it. The girl sometimes wished she could pull the stopper from the world and drain it like a bathtub. Alternatively she wished it were a head she could knock against a wall and give amnesia and that she could do so with each new memory the world developed. The world was always doing things that were not in anybody's best interest. After the fall, she sometimes woke at night from a throbbing in her arm, and she thought, I've just been lying on it wrong, and then she remembered. The pain medication made her want to earn enough money to buy her father a modest house in another country, a place she'd not be tempted to visit more than once a year.

One night, before her father joined the group that urged him to right the wrongs that drinking nightly to excess had inevitably wrought, and shortly after the death of his wife, the girl's father drank so much that he ended up in the hospital, "poisoned" was the word the doctor had used. This made the girl think of her father as a murder mystery, one starring a self-isolating man who lives alone on a remote island and eats dinner each night by the light of a candelabra. The man invites all perpetrators of his past unhappinesses to his drafty castle and dispatches each one in an improbable manner.

The girl could see in her father's yellowing skin that he had made an enemy of his body. One by one he would pick off his vital organs, against which he held long-smoldering resentments.

The next day, the girl wrote a note in her mother's hand that said, *Darling, I've never been one for happiness*, and she slipped it between Buddy Holly albums in her mother's room. Her father continued to drink and retch vigorously each night for the next several weeks, and one night, when the girl had had enough, she stood outside the door of his den and quietly hummed the melody of "That'll Be the Day." Then she sat on the sofa and watched a movie about lovers who were so star crossed, one could see their descendants for generations to come would be genetically doomed to all manner of romantic disappointment. After her father drained his glass, he padded heavily up the stairs. The girl, who felt she had recently arrived at key insights in her sleep—she couldn't recall them but believed nevertheless they equipped her with a potent cognition—divined the following, after the fact: her father went into the bedroom and pulled the Buddy Holly albums from the stack that leaned against the phonograph. The note fluttered to the floor like the petal of a fateful flower. The father picked it up and read it, and now with concrete evidence of his own consequence, proof that he was in fact a hazard to those who loved him, he felt a strange buoyancy in his body, as though he were losing mass, and he stumbled out of the room, down the stairs, and out of the house. Of course the girl didn't see her father find the note, and certainly she couldn't see what transpired, chemically or otherwise, in her father's mind and body, but she was good at deductive reasoning, Mr. Stratton had told her as much, and she knew when she saw his face, which seemed to float above his neck as he walked out the door, that this was precisely what had occurred.

The next day at school, the image of her mother's painted toenails appeared in the girl's mind, ten beads of blood arranged against the snowy backdrop of her imagination, as if an animal had pricked itself on a hidden barb and shambled across her thoughts, and she went into the girl's bathroom and applied red lipstick. She found Gregory Markovich between classes, pulled him into the empty gym, and said, "I've never been one for happiness." She thought if she were a character in a film, Bette Davis would surely be cast in the role of her. She thought it was one of the great human tragedies that dead actresses could not somehow be resurrected to star in roles for which they were absolutely perfect. How could anyone be certain, after all, that the role she was born to play would be conceived of in her lifetime? Gregory Markovich blinked at her uncertainly. The girl had considered becoming an actress herself, but the thought that the role she was biologically destined to play might not even be written until after her death made her suddenly realize how completely pointless such a life could turn out to be, and she got out her notebook to jot this down. She also noted the following: the fact that more rich people do not cryogenically preserve their bodies upon death shows a disappointing pessimism. Then she kissed Gregory Markovich, who'd been standing silently beside her as she wrote (the most important theories always have their unwitting accomplices), smack on the lips. She saw that Gregory Markovich's reaction to the kiss was the opposite of that of her father upon finding the note: she watched Gregory Markovich grow heavier, so resolutely heavy, in fact, that he made her think of a wrecking ball, or the waxing moon in full bloat, weightless but falling through space with the determination of a body no longer at rest, though he hadn't stirred at all, even during the kiss, and then Gregory Markovich sat on the gym floor, which caused the girl to cry. Not because this reaction suggested Gregory had not enjoyed the kiss—she certainly hadn't intended that—but because she knew that what had happened between them was going to do nothing at all to increase his popularity, and until that moment Gregory Markovich had been able to pretend otherwise. She recalled then her mother's list of lost things, recalled that number twenty-two, between *amethyst earring* and *rapidograph pen*, was *love*. The girl felt her own body grow heavy with loss, that kind of loss that comes from gain, like a boat taking on water. She knew she would eventually have no choice but to break her arm, and she stopped crying and sighed noisily.

When the girl first learned to write, her mother gave her an old steno pad and told her she should fill it with her thoughts, and this made the girl anxious, because what she liked to do most was sit and watch her dog sleep. She'd lay her head close to her dog's and think *rabbit, rabbit, rabbit,* and she'd wait for the dog's eyebrows and muzzle to begin to twitch, his feet to fidget. She didn't think she had as many thoughts in her head as other children, and she was afraid of being found out. The boy next door, whose mother was visibly pregnant one week and deflated the next, showed her a picture he'd cut out of a medical book of the ballooning head of a hydroencephalitic fetus, and he said if you looked inside, you'd find it empty. The girl imagined the baby's skull filled with the stillborn thoughts that would never make it into the world, and this caused her to get a stitch in her side, as though she'd run too long on an empty stomach. So the girl looked around the room and wrote *pillow, schnauzer, seashell, coin purse,* and although she knew these were not adequate thoughts, she thought in time these thoughts might fall in love and get married and have a child and buy a lawnmower, might fruitfully multiply, but then she thought about how you can cut a worm's body in half and make two wriggling worms, which the children in her neighborhood were always doing and which upset the girl very much. Despite the worm population seeming to double in number when you did this, she knew that the next day there would be fewer worms in the world than there had been the day before. And that's how she felt about recording her small thoughts, thoughts to which her teacher would assign a grade of *unsatisfactory*. But what made this a problem, one so potentially perilous it might one day even require a stay in the hospital, was the fact that as soon as she came to the last page in her notebook, an event that made her feel enormous relief as she contemplated giving up thinking entirely, another notebook appeared on her desk! A diabolically blank one, the notebook of a once-again thoughtless girl. It seemed there was no stopping the coming of these insatiable notebooks, and she held her dog's paw and pretended to count its heartbeats, the way her mother did when the girl was flushed with illness.

Years later, when the girl's father can no longer climb the stairs and moves to a condominium in a retirement community that insists the stucco exteriors of the buildings be painted in pastel colors, and whose clubhouse has a strict prohibition against the playing of bingo, he tells the girl, now a woman, that he believes it was his drinking that killed her mother. He pulls the woman to him and rests his soft chin on her head as he did when she was young, and she feels it judder with the force of long-repressed emotion surfacing. And the woman wonders, for the first time, if she should tell her father about the note. Some months ago, when she was packing her father's things for the move, she found, in a long-out-of-date atlas, a page from her last notebook that described the random and unlikely things that keep a person in the world and the random and unlikely things that cause a person to leave it, and this is a part of her theory that has proved to be true, the part that recognized that life wobbles along in a drunken manner, propelled by an unknowable engine, the part that understood it would have been unsurprising if, on that day long ago, she had chosen to fall from a much higher branch, just as it would have been unsurprising if she'd chosen to fall from a much lower branch, just as it would have been unremarkable if it *had* been her mother's arm by the side of the road, and it is this, after all, that is the origin of despair. Love, too, comes and goes like an empty bag snagged on a stiff wind, and because the distance between you and love, like the distance between a man and a clever tortoise, can always be halved, it is a destination that can never be reached. The woman knows her father's body is resting against hers, but she can feel only air around her, encircling the discrete container that shields the yearning soul from insurmountable intimacy.

The heart, however, is a hopeless invertebrate, and the woman gently urges her father into his club chair. She kneels in front of him, lays her crooked arm upon his knees, and they sit together in the winter light, which is both bright and grey at once, and recall, with the automatic fondness that gilds all distant recollection, how sweat had run from the girl's scalp and how the father had held her hand, her other hand, the one she wrote with, the one she'd meant to break, when the doctor removed the pins from her arm.

L'Enfant du Paradis

I was born a funambulist, fated to caper precariously across a taut cable. And what I gave my woebegone spectators—the sorrowful, who came to the theater in gray droves—was the ardent hope that they might witness the fall of one *petite pomme* from the tree, one tiny sadness plummeting at last to its conclusion. I'd fled the womb prematurely; tossed from the pot, truth be told, when I'd just reached a simmer, I came out half cooked. She who had grown impatient and expelled me took the trouble, however, to swaddle me in the severed toe of a stocking, and she dropped me into a teacup like a lump of sugar and delivered me to the rear entrance of the theater with this note: *Fell from the moon. Please feed.*

The manager of the Funambules, who trafficked theatrically in the willing gullibility of others, was briefly bedazzled by the idea of a demitasse of wriggling moonlight in his midst, and he turned me over in his hand, gurgled at me soothingly, *My little bumblebee, l'enfant de lune*, and then his eyes turned to glittering ingots, kaching!, when he saw in my miniaturization, my Tom Thumbery, great stage potential, and he flimflammed, by way of a promise of steady employment, a part-time contortionist newly arrived to town. He persuaded her to care for me and silence my shrill bleat, which she did, cleverly, with an eyedropper full of the nectar of flowers that suckle the hummingbirds. As I hungrily cheeped, Nathalie sang to me, *Au clair de la lune, mon ami Pierrot, prête-moi ta plume pour écrire un mot*. Sometimes for Pierrot she substituted the name the manager had begun to call me: Limoges, *fragile little Limoges*. But Nathalie feared I would succumb to my underdoneness, or, were I somehow to survive, would remain only a thimbleful and be crushed under the madding feet, so she found a charitable soul willing to help, and this Samaritan delivered me, fortuitously, across the ocean and into the hands of Dr. Teleborian, an ambitious pediatrician who longed to be the salvation of sickly infants.

As I was not a tiny, winged, vibratory creature, I could not be sustained by the sugar of rutilant flora for long, and he could see what I most needed in order to finish ripening into a sustainable boy was sterile warmth, and so he designed a glass oven that would provide shelter to prematurely evicted tenants like me and encourage our tiny hearts to blossom, help us gain the necessary amplitude for living. (Later, upon hearing the story of Hansel and Gretel, I would urge the siblings to leap willingly into the witch's oven, where I believed they would be baked into adults and made ready to return to the world, which they would find hostile and disagreeable, of course, but so it is. Until then, they would be safe from its rough vagaries in the warm, dark oven of childhood. The witch had been, it seemed to me, misunderstood, as warted women who live in forests often are.)

The prognosis for a featherweight such as myself was not at all favorable before Dr. Teleborian designed the baby hatchery, and hospitals were skeptical about the true efficacy of such a contraption, so Dr. Teleborian, soon to be the savior of half-baked foundlings everywhere, wisely decided to leave it up to the public, which always decides in favor of a spectacle after all, and he put us on display at the Pan-American Exposition in Buffalo, New York, next to the cyclorama that promised all on board a "Trip to the Moon" as it flapped its wings vertiginously.

Gawkers flocked and marveled at the tiny human beetles on their backs, kicking their twig legs in the air, in defiance of their puny beetle-hood, and sentimental spectators cooed at the hourly feedings. I believe some secretly rooted for our demise, so as to feel they'd gotten their nickel's worth, but there were those mothers or future mothers who wept upon our terrariums and howled with such sincere vigor that this became my inaugural memory—rain pinging against the roof—which explains why I have always felt a fond stirring in my breast during a thunderstorm.

Dr. Teleborian later confided to me in a letter that Leon Czolgosz, lonely, rumpled, aimless anarchist, possessing the brooding and solitary mien of one orphaned at birth, had visited the baby hatchery regularly, taking a particular shine to me. He had tapped on my window with a look of liberation in his eyes and broken into a sob only moments before pulling a revolver from his coat and assassinating President McKinley at the Temple of Music. I recall a vague feeling of incipient sorrow, and I do not doubt that it was on this afternoon that my empath's attraction to desolation sprang into being.

Despite this eclipsing national tragedy, we created such a sensation at the Expo that Dr. Teleborian set up at Coney Island a permanent sideshow of *Les Enfants du Paradis,* as we came to be known, alone in our glass mangers, shepherded into the world by grim-lipped nurses in stiff hats. Children screamed in the background, lofted into the air by a rickety roller coaster, and I grew anxiously, millimeter by millimeter, the smell of spun sugar reminding me of that first and saving supper. At night, I gazed out the window at the welling moon as it dribbled light upon the water.

Being a sickly spectacle is, whatever the outcome, necessarily a short-lived career, and so, my first performance a completed success—I lived and plumped, though I remained a runt loaf, was the toast of medical journals and also a shining symbol to the mothers of ailing infants of natal odds overcome—I soon found myself unemployed and back on the other side of the pond, inhaling once again the greasepaint of my beginning, wrapped in torn tulle and cradled in the worn cap of a gendarme, lying contentedly in the prop closet at the theater. I was made the charge of that part-time contortionist who had saved me, dear Nathalie. She was elated to see I was less comfortably cradled in the palm of her hand, and she was pleased to have steady work at last and a captive, if diminutive, audience. She stretched the eager taffy of her body, twisted it into cheerful shapes, and made me howl with infant delight. She fed me crusts sopped in warm milk from the tap-dancing goats, the pickled eggs of skylarks, and a gruel she concocted from the vendors' confections, and she let me chew on the chiffon sash of her costume.

Such a diet was sure to make of me an antic and jovial fellow who could balance himself on the fine rope of a silk thread she thought, perhaps make of me even an aerialist or a star-eyed mime who conjures hilarity and sorrow from thin air. *I only wish Maman had fed me such gay cuisine, Limoges,* said Nathalie, with a distant dreaminess as she lay on her stomach and rounded her body into a C, piloted each spoonful into my mouth with her foot.

All the Funambules took an interest in me. I was their kith, chipped from the moon, which they believed to be their country of origin, moonlight the substance that coursed through their veins, and I walked first on my hands and then on a briskly rolling ball and finally, grudgingly, on two feet across a dull, unmoving landscape.

When I grew to the height of a bucket, I began to juggle: first buttons, then boysenberries, then tree toads, who, although cooperative, were so dizzy afterward they lay on their backs, paddled the air, then quickly fell to snoring, as toads that have gotten into the beer barrel will do. My industry pleased the stage manager, who waggled his unpruned shrub of a moustache at Nathalie and appeased her considerable sweet tooth with a lusciously pink, three-tiered torte, the very color of the silk pantaloons the danseuse who pirouetted on the backs of galloping pigs, wore, pink as a hungry tongue.

As I gained sovereignty over my modestly lengthening limbs, each performer attempted to recruit me for his specialty: there was the man with the feathered legs, whose stovepipe hat no gale force could knock from his bald head—Abraham Chicken he was christened; the twins, Amelie and Garance, conjoined at the wrist, who inhaled so deeply and widely that they flattened the flesh of their abdomens into a sail, leapt in the air with the grace of sugar gliders, and lilted like a slip of paper to the ground; the cat girl, Yvette, who sprang onto window ledges and ignored everyone she met; Madame Mondieu, the woman who read tragedies from the newspaper aloud, turning its pages with her toes as she balanced a corpulent man atop the palm of each hand; the tumblers, who somersaulted up walls easy as blown tumbleweeds but toppled to the ground whenever they tried to traverse a level surface; and Nathalie, of course, who looped herself into words, one after the other, contorting into a story, her body's memoir: *There . . . once . . . was . . . a . . . girl . . . with . . . arms . . . so . . . long . . . they . . . required . . . their . . . own . . . bed . . . their . . . own . . . place . . . at . . . the . . . table. . . .*

At the end of each performance, she twisted my feet, angled my legs, dotted the i with my head, and held me up to the audience—*Le Fin*—and there was something about the sight of my stunted boy's limbs cursively knotted for the spectators' entertainment that caused them to cheer and burst into tears and toss lilies at our feet. That first night, Nathalie found a gilded birdcage full of the finest bonbons at her dressing table, and every night after a new and enchanting confection. Later, over the course of the years, her body, that mutineer, would turn against her, its script becoming unreadable, its swollen symbols spilling illegibly (eventually she would give up her lexical contortions and would take up, instead, swallowing to the hilt the water-whetted bill of a swordfish), but the stage manager loved her all the more unbound, and she was happy to lie flat as a loosened ribbon and let her bones and flesh unspool at last, to burgeon in all directions for him.

Eventually, I grew to be a young man, though my body's ambitions remained petite—half of me had been left behind on the moon, I liked to think—and I could stand without bending beneath the muzzle of the manager's borzoi. Nathalie said, *It is time, Limoges, for you to decide what sort of artiste you were meant to be, aerosaltant, funambulist, sword swallower, contortionist? You will be a grand success, Limoges, whatever you choose. There is a brilliance in your blood.* My blood. I tried to smile but felt my mouth assume a rueful twist. She guided my eyes with her gaze to the night sky, which slumbered dimly.

The War to Preserve Civilization had raged across Europe and left it in tatters and made us uncertain as to the future. We all groped for understanding, filled with grim questions about the state of humanity, and looked toward jollity and work to avert our eyes from the terrible answers. Although I knew I belonged to the stage, I did not feel I had yet found my true calling, the use to which my moon-birthed body was meant to be put. One night, as I puzzled silently over my future, I sat with the singing mule, Marcel, who was always in his cups and rife with sorrow as soon as the sun set, and we sang sad songs in the moonlight and raised our steins to despair. Marcel was quite a good tenor, but his considerable talent only made the audience suspicious, and sometimes they hopped onto the stage and tugged skeptically at his ears. A mule who carries a tune rather than a saddlebag is always, in this world of lead, an object of incredulity. *No one knows the burden of being a melodic mule,* sobbed Marcel, *except you, Limoges, you understand,* and he thanked me for lightening his load.

Occasionally Marcel was joined by Guillaume, the mysophobic pig, who suffered from painful hoof bunions due to ill-fitting galoshes. He would not walk upon the mud of the world without them, however, and all the world seemed a sty to Guillaume. He longed to be one of the backs upon which Giselle, the silk-draped, high-stepping equestrienne, capered, but because the boots caused him to move at a stumbling gallop, he once tossed Giselle into the orchestra pit, so he'd been placed on furlough until he kicked his repulsion of dirt and could trot more languidly with the others. Guillaume's somber mug drooped to the ground. There is nothing so mournful as an enterprising pig without purpose.

Tonight Marcel leaned his head against Guillaume, laid his ears consolingly across the pig's pink noggin, and some disgruntled stagehand spoiling for a hey rube happened by and snarled, "Well, if it ain't the hog and pony show." The warm and rancid gusting of a drunken guffaw was followed by this dull barb: "You make the cyclops cry!" Marcel could deliver a blow that would take the bluster out of the most belligerent roustabout, but I urged him to tilt his ears away from the taunt and rise above it, and he and Guillaume turned their heads nobly to the side and watched the lout stumble home. They quickly after fell to snoring, and I stroked Marcel's handsome ears.

After I left those two, I approached the room of The Bearded Man. His act was unpopular, and so he'd had to learn to dodge the welting wallop of a lobbed cabbage. He could grow hair on his face at will and at an impressive velocity too, and on a good day he could take anatomical requests—could fur up his legs, his arms, his back on demand—and would lumber about with the famished grace of a bear recently roused from hibernation, but invariably the crowd was full of traditionalists, who preferred their beards to sprout only from the chins of fine ladies, an obstinate prejudice The Bearded Man had long combatted, and they heckled him nightly with such fervor he tried to will a womanly welling in his pectorals: to no avail. His pariah-hood made him weep when alone.

As I reached his door, I bent to the keyhole and breathed deeply the humid air of sorrow, and shortly thereafter I heard his head drop to his pillow, heard the snuffling of contented sleeping. This had all made for a taxing evening, and I poured myself into bed. The Funambules were a stormy troupe, but I had come to see over the course of my life that the winds whistled less plaintively in my presence, and taming the tempest was, for the moment, avocation enough.

About this time, a reporter from an American newspaper came to the theater and asked if he might have a moment of my time. Mr. Jonathan Albright, crack journalist, sat across from me with his fedora tipped jauntily back and a hungry wetness behind his ears, and informed me that Dr. Teleborian, with whom I'd regrettably lost touch, had recently fallen ill and died. He saw my face droop toward my lap and said, "Aw, sorry to be the messenger, kiddo, thought you knew," and he scribbled a note to himself.

Then he told me that in the course of plotting the trajectory of the doctor's career for his obituary, he'd begun to research the years of the baby hatchery and had discovered this: I was the only surviving participant from that original experiment! My eyes rounded, and he said, "Also a news flash, eh?" Another jotting. But this was not the most alarming news the journalist would deliver to me that day. He told me that it was *not* the case that my siblings hadn't flourished in the tropics of our incubation. On the contrary, the tiny glass gardens of our personal Edens had saved nearly all of us, and so impressive was the survival rate of these prematurely born babies, the sort of wee creatures who, previously, had come into the world only to quickly find it fatal, that hospitals everywhere had since adopted the technology and made Dr. Teleborian an internationally fêted success and earned him a tidy fortune to boot. No, the glass-garden babies had thrived and grown and indeed all the others had exceeded my humble stature considerably; I was by far the most minute of the lot. I angled my head in a way that must have communicated to Mr. Albright that this was not startling information he'd uncovered, and he said, "Old news, gotcha," jot-jot.

"Okay, well, get a load of this," said Mr. Albright, and here he began to confide to me a story that seemed to fill the air around us with a fine ash. "Your Coney Island cronies, most of 'em, grew up, sure, but here's what you're probably not wise to: every last one of those melancholy babies eventually met their maker in a tragic-like manner. But wait," he swiveled his head around as if he were in danger of being scooped, "that ain't the half of it, brother." He leaned toward me confidentially. "Not only did these doomed mopes cash in their chips in spectacular fashion—" here he whistled and provoked a distant echo from the illusionist's parrot, which made him lower his voice—"everyone who had the misfortune to stand within spitting distance of your cursed brethren on the day of their demise went home that night not on the 6:05 but in a pine box, if you follow me." I didn't and felt my face furrow with befuddlement. "It's a big bass to swallow, I know. But picture this: trainwreck, fatal contagion, earthquake, mining accident, buckling bridge, crazy cataclysms of every stripe! Each of your fellow heat-hatched former peewees were walking around ignorant as faulty wiring to the calamity they would one day be at the center of, each one of them the eye of a gathering disaster just waiting to blink." Mr. Albright's face, fittingly somber throughout, brightened at the end, and he pulled the pencil from behind his ear and began again his stenography. Then he sighed, shook his head, and erased what he'd written.

I'd heard about the tragedy of poor Mary Goldstein, who died clutching a shirtwaist in her young hand when the factory went up in a blaze, but Dr. Teleborian had been careful not to let news of the doomed destinies of the rest of the hothouse brood reach me. As I turned this troubling tale over in my mind, I felt myself become unmoored and begin to float, and though it was only an imagined feeling, I knew if I simply lifted my heels it would be much more than mere mental mirage. I knew at that moment I could lift myself toward the rising moon I watched as it crept up the sky outside the window. I believed, however, that lifting into the air at a moment such as this would be the height of impertinence, so I remained tethered to the ground by force of will, which, Newton's conjecture notwithstanding, is all gravity truly amounts to if you ask me.

His face took on a look of almost paternal concern, and he said, "I know, it all sounds like banana oil, but it gets loonier. So before the doom and disaster, while your comrades were ripening into adults, seems they were all, boys and girls alike, thin skinned, ready yowlers every one of 'em, impressionable as putty, taking the heaviness of the world onto their little shoulders, but, unlike Atlas, they were often crushed by the sorrow around them. You only have to open a newspaper to see that sopping up sorrow's a mug's game, no end to it. Family after family told me the same story, their little Johnny or Evelyn sensitive as an exposed nerve. Little suffering Jesuses on the cross, if you'll pardon my saying so, but without, well, without the same, erm, sponsorship I guess you'd say, no sense of purpose. I think they were poisoned by their own pointless sensitivity, by being 'tender as a chicken' as my father would say, just before he plucked from my neck a feather or two and kicked me in the tail feathers." Mr. Albright paused his excited theorizing and looked at me quizzically. "But then there's you," he said. "You, Limoges—can I call you Limoges?—the sole surviving hatchling!" Then Mr. Jonathan Albright blink-blinked and asked, with a look of searching sincerity stretching his face, "So what do you think? Got a hunch? It's a doozy of a mystery, Limoges, a great cosmic whodunit, and you're the key to it!"

He continued his eager inquisition, certain I must have some sleeping insight, a hypothesis as to why the children nurtured in the shining hatchery of hope that had made its debut at the Pan-American Exposition in Buffalo, New York, why all but one, and he was polite enough not to look at me accusingly as he spoke, had met with an untimely expiration.

As I gazed upon his expression of yearning bafflement, into my mind came the face of Leon Czolgosz, anarchist wannabe and assassin, with that look of bewildered sorrow and fury, and I began to glimpse my own purpose. And try as I might to cast my gaze elsewhere, I could not stop the mechanism of thought from grinding forward. The ambitious obituarist watched my face closely as the cogs of this grudging understanding whirred frantically behind it, and I left Mr. Jonathan Albright with a puzzled expression still crimping his brow, a look that suggested he'd seen the world begin to tilt.

That night, as I sat with Marcel, each of us silently nursing a quandary to which there seemed no solution, I stroked his weary ears, so full of the vituperations of skeptics, and began to think again about the hatchery. I decided to confide in Marcel what Mr. Jonathan Albright had revealed to me during our conversation. I thought perhaps it might cheer him to think there could be an even less fortunate creature in the world than a singing mule. I so longed to antidote Marcel's dejection.

As I recounted the story, Marcel shook his head and his eyes welled sympathetically. I should have known a soul as fine as Marcel's would find no relief in my desolation. He sniffed and sneezed, and I looked at the beer foam circling his muzzle. I daubed at his nose with my handkerchief and thought about the oxygen pumped into each of the hatchery chambers, oxygen that had come from outside the building, Dr. Teleborian being a firm believer in the power of fresh air to revivify an ailing body, but there was something . . . unsettling about that exposition air, a memory of which still pricks my nose to this day. Something about the overly roasted sweetness of it filled a body with a sense of preemptive loss and futility, as if being born were itself beside the point.

I mentioned this to Marcel, and he said something that struck me as passing wise. He said, "Too much hope, Limoges, can curdle an atmosphere sure as the sun can clabber a pail of cream." And it was true, surely a glittering desperation surrounds any exhibition that trumpets the arrival of a bright futurity. The air our struggling bodies had imbibed was thick and fetid with that frantic insistence that civilization was *not* hurtling toward its end, no! Rather it was headed toward perfectability, can't you see? Unsightly squalor, inconvenience, inefficiency were all soon to be consigned to history, hooray! Mortality itself would prove to be no formidable opponent for the ingenuity of man, his machines, his pharmacon, his moonward ambitions! "That air you inhaled, Limoges," said Marcel, "it was filled with a desperately hopeful attar that lilted across the world in those years preceding that great and grisly war to come."

We infants on display at the Pan-American Exposition of Buffalo, New York, had been nursed on a highly concentrated formula of expectation. Robust, garden-variety newborns, on the other hand, who are suckled as God intended, drink in the sorrow of new mothers, which is substantial (the mothers already anticipating, as they are, the eventual decrepitude and death of these new initiates), and in that way they actually immunize themselves against crushing despair. I ran this by Marcel, and he hiccupped and finished my reasoning for me: "But a body fed on accidental hope is a fetching temptress to Sorrow." And so the Children of Paradise, no immunities to protect them, would later attract to themselves the world's misery so decisively that a vortex would open up around each and lure destruction to him with tornadic force.

"The treachery of the optimistic oxygen on which we were nourished explains my fellow fingerlings' doomed beginnings, but what to make of me, Marcel, my persistence?" What of *fragile little Limoges*, who routinely inhaled the desolation of the Funambules but had thus far skirted catastrophe? This puzzle was too much for the both of us, and dear Marcel, who woefully regretted ever hearing those first bittersweet strains of concertina music that made him sit up and sing with a sentimental sweetness known to leave even the most cynical auditor salting his absinthe, leaned his head against mine and began to snore. I looked up at the grinning moon, half of whose waning face was concealed, and wondered what it was I was meant to do with this spared life of mine, this puny but resilient body.

Unable to fall asleep, I continued to reason it out in my head, and it occurred to me that I had been spared partly because, as the only motherless urchin in the group, having been booted from the womb at an untimely age and donated to the stage, I had come into the world without the burden of even the faintest expectation—for me that first breath and every one thereafter was a fond surprise—and so, feeling no entitlement to growth, I, motherless runt, did not insist on it and aspired only to bald survival. My next thought was accompanied by both a bracing clarity and my mind's sad-sack portrait of that angry anarchist whose favor I had enjoyed, champion of the have-nots (and who had then had less than I?): my true salvation was the immunities that had been bolstered by the furious desolation of Leon Czolgosz, an influence so potent it had slipped the seal of the glass and infected me sure as polio. There is nothing, I suddenly realized, so inoculating as the sorrow of a reluctant insurgent. While I, like the others, had been denied the immunization of mother's milk, I had imbibed something even more invigorating under the circumstances: Leon Czolgosz and his anarchistic grief had fathered my insusceptibility to the endless rue and injustice that distinguish the world as the world.

The question that now faced me was this: what was I to do with my imperviousness to the world's pain? How best could I honor the memory of those infants incubated in sorrow, *Les Enfants de la Tragédie*, whose only mistake had been to be born too small in a world built for lumbering Molochs?

Thus began my career as a sorrow swallower.

So I went to Nathalie and told her what I at last understood my calling to be, and she spoke with the stage manager, who was not at first enthusiastic, given the unpredictability and possible liabilities of involving the audience in a performance. He'd been cautious about such acts ever since he'd had to let go the mesmerist from whose hypnotic influence some volunteers never awoke. It was later revealed that the mesmerist was an incurable insomniac, who hadn't slept since his fourth birthday and whose wild longing for unconsciousness crept unwittingly into his enchantments. I assured the stage manager that it was my intention to lift from the body some of the weight of misfortune, not to add to it, but I understood his hesitation.

During the time of my childhood, the three-dimensional (four- if you counted Pascal, the unusually aerodynamic chicken who pro- vided the wings for Time's Wingèd Chariot, which he filled with broken pocket watches, and darted invisibly from stage to balcony in an eyeblink then back again), life-sized entertainments offered by the Funambules were increasingly being abandoned for the flat- ter projections of the Kinetoscope parlors, the nickelodeons, the cinema. Audiences gasped and cheered at the Lumières' lassoing of motion on film, Méliès' aeronautical wizards rocketing into space and blinding the right eye of the Man in the Moon (a phantasm I found objectionable, though I was riveted and could not turn my head from the screen for a second—my heart leapt at the sight of the molten face of my father. Ah, such high hopes had I for *Voyage dans la Lune!*).

Monsieur Méliès was, in the early days, a frequent visitor to the Funambules and for a time courted Nathalie and begged her to twist herself into the shape of his name reclining in the crook of a quarter moon. His *very special effect*, he called her. But Nathalie had eyes only for the stage manager, and the famed cinemagician, crestfallen, tipped his hat, bowed to his rival, and abandoned his amorous pur- suit. Some years later, after his film company went bankrupt, he be- came a toy salesman and one night returned to leave behind in Nathalie's dressing room a bendable doll shaped into the word *étoile*, clearly an homage to the once rubber-boned body of the woman whose contortions he'd adored.

So our plundered accounts had recently incised the stage man- ager's face with deep ravines of worry, and, out of desperation to rescue the show from the almshouse and put food in the growling bellies of its performers, he agreed to give my sorrow swallowing a trial run.

The workaday stupor-dispelling spectacle people truly long to see is something that smacks of the tragic, a devastating event they can observe, at a safe distance of course, as it assails another human being. They do not wish to hear about it secondhand. They desire to see their own private suffering swollen in the breast of a stranger to the point of deformity, ruination, death, to be its witness, its spectator, to not be the pullet whose neck is being wrung. I had of course no intention of satisfying this appetite for the blood of others, but I knew such thirsts must somehow be slaked and believed it could be done to the profit of the blood-parched, which is to say all of us. It was my hope that if humanity were to watch not a tragedy in the making but a great sadness relived, see it streak down the cheeks of the unfortunate, a change could be wrought in its wolfish heart. Such cravings might be abandoned entirely when the audience beheld a fellow mortal eating the pain of another whole, like a bad oyster, watched him draw it down the gullet and swallow it into extinction. This digestion of sorrow might liberate us, I thought, from the secret pleasure we all take in watching that head roll at our feet, congratulating ourselves as we do at such moments for not being, this time, the tender neck that has been cleaved by the ravenous blade of the guillotine. And after all, though any day we are not beheaded is a good one, it is only a momentary escape.

The stage manager believed mere sorrow swallowing would not be enough to lure the only vaguely curious off the street, and since there was a vacancy for a tightrope walker, his last funambulist having developed destabilizing hammertoes, we decided I should conduct my consumption of the world's multifarious afflictions precariously aloft.

The first funambulistic swallowing began with little fanfare, only this introduction solemnly intoned by Nathalie: *Limoges the Delicate will now, with the towering fearlessness and grandeur of spirit his wee body conceals, trip intrepidly across . . . the Tightrope of Fate! Having arrived at his destiny, he will then take into his fragile breast, like boiling water into a teacup, a great sadness, and there he will steep it until he has absorbed the melancholia and liberated the pained heart of the weight of its torment! Will it be your pain the Swallower of Sorrow funnels into the bottle of the world's ills he carries inside him?*

As I stepped my toe to the twine upon which I would inch, I cast my gaze briefly toward the audience, and there, illumined by the false twilight of the theatre, were haggard faces in the grip of an ennui it would take no small sensation to antidote. They looked upon me with disaffection, thinking, perhaps, that a body as light and compact as mine mincing about on a fine thread was neither surprising nor alarming. Were I to bumble and pitch off the rope, I'd be little more than a fallen feather wisping silently to the ground and would cause a good deal less excitement than the doughy splat of a buxom aerialist, which is what they truly longed to see. I would have to take on weight if I were going to capture their attention.

The calliope sang out, and I wavered forward to the gay twittering of "Entry of the Gladiators." I looked below at the sawdust scattered about the stage and knew that, despite my stalled body, I would likely not flutter to safety were I to topple. But I understood that the only way to interest the audience in my derring-do was to reassure them that bones would break and blood would pour forth and irrigate the stage with my momentary notoriety if I stumbled, and they'd be there to witness it through splayed fingers, pretending to avert their eyes from the thrilling spectacle. I looked down to Nathalie, who cheered me on with clasped hands raised in the air, then up at the wooden moon and stars dangling from wires above me, and I stepped on my heel with willful imprecision. I wobbled, dropped, clenched the rope between my buttocks and fists, and I spun like a child's toy, a whirligig, a teetotum, spun like the dial of the scale upon which the fat lady sat to prove she was not merely an inflatable colossus, whirled like a weathervane in a mistral, until the momentum slowed and the propeller of my body came to rest, feet twisted tightly together in the air. This was a practiced maneuver and I regretted that I had to sink to such theatrics in order to rouse onlookers from the coma of their boredom, but rouse them I did! Shrieks rose in the air and men leapt to their feet, no doubt to get a better gander at the coming carnage. After a few more tentative revolutions, I righted myself and rose shakily once again to a standing position. The audience was now attentively silent, and I nodded to Nathalie, who moved to stand on the apron of the stage.

Limoges the Delicate, she said to the hushed audience, *whom the Moon himself delivered to our doorstep, can influence the tidal*

pull of the sorrow in which we all swim, and he now wishes to draw
that sorrow into his breast so as to bring about the ebbing of grief.
Nathalie asked would a sad volunteer please step forward. She suggested that the more ponderous the pain, the more elevating the outcome, and she entreated the most desolate among them to become buoyancy's inaugural recruit. Heads wagged discreetly as the spectators scanned the crowd to see who was willing to risk being made the butt of high buffoonery. The memory of the mesmerist and his permanently afflicted volunteers clearly lingered in the minds of the theatregoers: mouths yawned, arms crossed, eyes darted suspiciously. The Funambules' patrons had troubles enough without being made to moo or bleat or snuffle or nicker at inopportune moments.

Nathalie had anticipated this and told me if we were patient and steeled our nerves against the audience's hesitation, there would eventually be one whose leaden heart would impel him to shamble forward, one whose suffering far exceeded the prospect of public foolishness, and so I waited and wobbled encouragingly, and, after a good deal of scattered coughing and much squeaking of seats, a sorrowful person at last stood up and walked with doleful exactitude to the stage. Nathalie took the woman's hand and guided her to the ladder that would lead this mournful madame to the platform and to me. When she reached the top, I pivoted on the rope and stepped back in her direction.

The woman's face was heavy with wide eyes, eyes made large, I imagined, by a trying circumstance, rather than by a bloodline's imprint, eyes that made me think of chasms into which things have accidentally fallen, pooling darknesses a passerby cannot help but gaze into even though she knows the fallen objects have been lost to her forever. Her face was youthful and aged at once, fine skin etched with a sadness that seemed as jagged and intractable as the Pyrenees.

I touched her chin. "Speak to me of your sorrow," I said, "and I will do what I can to drink it." I put my mouth to hers, and there was a contagion of tittering in the audience, but the woman did not blanch. I could see she held out little hope for the promise of such a purging, but she spoke, her lips fluttering against mine like moths, and I felt my heart thump-thumping in my stomach.

She told me her husband had been missing for many months and was presumed to be lying dead amidst other fallen men, in a field strewn with the bodies of soldiers, compatriots and enemies alike. She said she dreamt of him looking, during the conclusive beats of his heart, into the final eyes his mind would record: the eyes of the man who had taken his life, the eyes of a man whose life he had taken. All around the dead and dying men was the vibration of artillery and gunfire—she could feel it throb in her own dreaming face—but there was no hearing left to register the reports. There were only the distant dreams of widowed women. "And that's just how the world trundles along, isn't it?" she said, her own eyes two moons darkening into the annihilation of a new cycle.

She said everywhere around her husband and his enemy were pairs of men, all neatly aligned, face to face, knee to knee, looking rapt, like a field full of lovers whose mutual gaze cannot be sundered as they lie for the first night in their marriage bed, stunned to share the heat of a body they long to both kiss and cradle. She told me her son had spoken no word since the last news they'd had of his father.

I swallowed as she spoke, drank in the dolor with parched vigor, as if after days of traveling in the desert I had come suddenly upon a freshet, and when I finished lapping up every droplet of her grief, I felt a stitch in my side, felt an ache begin to beat in my liver. But quickly after, my body began to granulate, I felt infinitesimal space open up between its particles, and I had to curl my toes around the rope to keep from rising up. The woman's face went still and blank as a pail of water and I saw air slip beneath her feet and lift her a pea's width into the air. Though the rising was slight, the audience perceived the lightening as well and raised their hands to their mouths as the woman backed down the ladder, feet cushioned by the air that now held her in its hand. I walked with clutching toes to the center of the rope, Nathalie moved behind me, and with one final gulp I sank and fell backward, landed in her arms. I looked above me to the crescent moon that hung in the stage sky and saw that they'd neglected to paint the backside.

The audience remained silent until Nathalie carried me into the wings, and then as if the lit fuse of the performance had finally reached the powder keg, the crowd detonated, screams and wild applause ringing out of the building and into the streets for the next quarter of an hour.

In the weeks that followed, moping lines of spectators-in-waiting filled the streets outside the theater before every performance. Throngs of hard-luckers hung their heads and waited mournfully, harboring only the tiniest flea of hope, a faint itch at the base of their necks, a modestly nursed belief that they might be delivered from their despair. Although there was occasional resentment on the part of my confreres about the overshadowing popularity of my sorrow swallowing, the prosperity that accompanied it and the brimming bellies and downy bedding it afforded the troupe stroked all hoisted hackles back in place.

Nathalie's contentment, however, was not so easily purchased. Since giving up the stage, Nathalie had devoted herself to my high-wire sorrow swallowing, but as she watched me grow wan as daybreak, she began to regret her enthusiasm for my act, and she fretted over the toll each night's ingestion was taking on my slackening body, sorrow an improper diet, she said, for building a roseate robustness of constitution. When we'd hatched this act, neither of us had realized its consequences. Each afternoon when she renewed her objections, my mind drifted to thoughts of my famously incubated siblings and their vulnerability to the world's bottomless despair, and I knew that, though I was able to cork the vessel inside me once I'd drunk my fill, the seal was not a tight one and I was not immune to the effects of the leakage. After every performance, the pain in my side pulsed a little more sharply. Nevertheless, I found myself each afternoon so parched, thirsting for the dejection that moistened the cheeks of every secretly hopeful audience member, that I was helpless not to open my mouth and quaff down the dark draft every evening. Each night, my body a little closer to its absence, I slept fitfully, but I pictured myself walking into the mouth of the moon and tried not to think about the price such a journey would exact.

After two months, my body had grown increasingly insubstantial, and Nathalie and the stage manager began to quarrel. There had been tension between them ever since the stage manager hired a new contortionist, Odile, to whom Nathalie discovered he'd sent bonbons after an especially elastic performance. All contortionists, it seems, are plagued by a sweet tooth whose overindulgence can lead to an early retirement, as in the case of Nathalie. The stage manager had always pushed the plate of profiteroles in Nathalie's direction, perhaps fearful his own ballooning belly and thickening haunches would set her eyes to wandering (the stage manager, not a handsome man, was never quite able to trust that Nathalie was as loyal and dependable as the sun, which is always there, even in the most dun and drizzly gloom, always ready to rise and relieve the moon of its duties). Nathalie insisted there be at least rejuvenating interludes between my performances and scolded the stage manager, saying it was his duty to protect me—I was practically flesh of his flesh after all—but the stage manager blustered, "Oh, my dear, be reasonable! Limoges has had a bilious complexion since birth, and there isn't meat enough on those petite bones for him truly to be imperiled—he survived the heartlessness of his own early expulsion and abandonment after all!" At this, Nathalie's face fell and darkened mournfully, she, too, a deeply sensitive soul.

"Andandand anyway, it isn't as though any true poison is passed to that boy from the heartsore glum Guses that mob the theater every night!" As his words spilled out, he shivered his body like a defiant goose straightening his feathers, but he was unable to look into Nathalie's eyes as he spoke, and his gaze came to rest instead on the tips of his shoes. Nathalie's face fell like an aerialist made careless by heartache, and both the stage manager and I could see that such a suggestion, that I was engaged in mere theatrics, was an even greater betrayal than his consorting with another bendable grisette. The stage manager fluttered again, emitted a petulant growl, then stole a glance at Nathalie to see how he'd fared. Nathalie turned with a limpid grace that recalled her earlier days and walked away to the dressing room of Madame Mondieu, who would regale her with stories of the day's catastrophes. I watched the stage manager's face alternate between indignant resolve and forlorn regret, then he waddled with unconvincing élan toward the room in which Odile sat coiled like a cobra waiting to be charmed.

In the days that followed, I shrank, and Nathalie, so as to entertain me, ignored the arthritic stiffening that labored her movements, perhaps hoping I might forget that the world outside the theater throbbed with heartache. "The main attraction deserves a little divertissement now and then," she said and smiled, petting my nose. She spent her evenings bending herself into poems and tales she'd memorized for me. *Who stirs the sea? wondered the Sultana, gazing out the window. It comes not from the diving cormorants nor from stones fallen from the wall. See there the heaving sacks from which sobs break free? They sound the flood that floats them on, moving their sides like human forms. Look, Limoges, how serene the moon that plays on the sea.* With that I looked out the window into the sky just as my maker mantled himself in the wandering gauze of night.

Nathalie and the stage manager were now interminably at odds, and one night she begged me to leave the Funambules, to run away with her, to flee to the Orient, the North Pole, to America, any remote locale into whose excess we might disappear like two hares into a forest, a place whose sorrows could be dissolved by other means, where she would feed me proper victuals and knit a tiny scarf to warm my throat, and I could soak her feet at night like a proper son. "Would that not give you purpose enough, Limoges, the leavening of sorrow one limb at a time, lifting the day's weight from your dear Nathalie's ankles?" Nathalie's eyes gained a heaviness, for she knew I was paralyzed by an insatiable longing no aching extremities could satisfy.

Shortly after this entreaty, Mr. Jonathan Albright appeared once again at my door. I suspected Nathalie had summoned him, had enlisted his aid in coaxing me to abandon my "self-sabotaging mission to still the world's clamorous cri de coeur," but I was happy to see him, he the one person who knew and might comprehend the origin of my errand.

We sat on the front row of the theater and gazed upon the rope I would creep across that night. "So, Limoges, you've become something of a sensation since our last chin-wag."

I was stunned by Jonathan's weather-beaten appearance, his rumpled suit, and the gravel of his sleep-deprived voice. He looked a good ten years older than the last time we met, and the skin below his eyes bore the gray smudge of a troubled soul. He noted my searching stare and said, "I know I look a bit of a mess. Probably appear to you a tad zozzled, but it's not like that. Little trouble at home, that's all." He ran his hands through his disheveled hair. "I married a swell gal, Limoges, Junie. Junie Albright, don't that sound fine?" He smiled dreamily. "I met her while I was digging up the goods on the Expo experiment. She's the sister of one of your hatchery mates. Her brother Philip was the last to die, tornado in Mattoon, Illinois, where he was passing through. Philip was a restless wanderer, traveling from farm to farm in search of day labor, just enough to keep him in bread and sausage and get him to the next town. Always kept in touch with Junie, though. They found her picture in the rubble." He leaned forward, arms on his knees. "She took it real hard, and when I showed up, asking questions about her brother, her parents told me to beat it at first, but then she started showing me pictures of Philip as a boy, and her family said she shone more brightly than she had since her brother died two years before. We wed the following summer.

"Lately, though, she's stopped sleeping, and she's started walking at night. She heads toward the train tracks, climbs the water tower, walks to the river. It's as if . . . as if she's trying to join the Great Majority, Limoges!" He clutched my shoulder, and I laid my hand upon his.

His stricken look gave way to a half laugh and he leaned again upon his knees, clasped his hands. "Aw, geez, Limoges, here I am running off at the kisser when it's you I came to hear about. You got your sympathetic ear turned toward the wretched masses every night, up to your eyebrows in sob stories a good deal sadder'n mine I bet. I can see it isn't much agreeing with you, kid." He gave me that parental look I recognized from our previous conversation.

"This act of yours, it's admirable, Limoges, truly it is, but it's eating you head to tail, I can see it."

"Just one ravened bone to another, eh?" I said and smiled. Jonathan did his best to hitch his own mouth into a grin, and he shook his head. Looking at the startling grief-mottled skin of Jonathan Albright, I finally had to concede what I had not been quite able to bring myself to confront, for what other avocation could there be for a body suspended in becoming? I'd felt I could ill afford to eye the enterprise of my swallowing too closely. Nevertheless, Jonathan and Nathalie were right; each performance was inching me closer to the days of the hatchery, when my body, the size and complexion of a lima bean, had struggled, against odds and prognostications, to flourish. I wondered what Dr. Teleborian would think of me now. Would he pronounce me a deferred failure, a doomed runt, whose extinction a revolutionary invention could only forestall? (But then again was that not the history of the world, mortality the disease we all succumb to in time? As Marcel once said to me, "The dead do not sob, Limoges. We must weep while we can." I'd been aware of my proximity to the end since my beginning. My trek, like Junie Albright's, was an expedited one perhaps, but were we not all headed in the same direction?) And my hatchery kith, would their sad lives, the tragic permeability of their skins, be for naught, all cross and no salvation? I knew my stomach would never hold so much sorrow that I could swallow a sadness completed, reverse an ill-fated outcome, digest and void the long history of animal misery, but with increasing urgency I felt, in my joints and my teeth, in my kidneys and coccyx, the onus of my experimental infancy, and I saw little point to a life, however brief, spent not trying to lend the injured what feeble succor I could.

"Nathalie loves you, Limoges. That's something to stick around for, innit? Innit?" Jonathan's pleading tone, the lines of exhaustion that aged his face, made me doubt my muddled convictions. Was my consumption of sorrow only further feeding that of those I loved?

And what of love, sorrow's intimate? Love was something I felt so forcefully, with such a swelling sense of debt, even thinking the word caused my blood and breathing to slow to a perilous crawl. "I love Nathalie," I said quietly, love her with the devoted ardor a sickly duckling, left for dead and lying on his back, feels for the first star that falls into his eye when he cracks open his gaze. As for the sort of love that makes the bosom and loins flutter in tandem, I had long ago come to understand that, in the heart that houses the world's gnawing grief, there is no room for romantic enchantment. Perhaps that sacrifice was my strategy: if I nurtured the kernel of my own paltry sorrow until it grew to the size of the moon, that ravenous Moloch that is the woebegone world might be appeased and allow the innocents, the good hearts, the well-meaning, those most undeserving of torment, that is, the Nathalies and Jonathans and Junies, the Marcels and Guillaumes, the war widows and premature infants of the world, might allow them to know nothing of suffering.

Jonathan Albright, love-grizzled seer, could see through my thin skull to the thoughts tossing inside and said, "You can't save us all, Limoges." I reached my hand out toward his smarting chest, and he placed it back against my own.

That night, Nathalie came into my dressing room and knelt at my feet. She had spoken with Jonathan Albright. She pointed to the ghostly face that stared at me from the mirror, moved her own next to mine, and her reflection begged me to cancel my performance. "Soon, Limoges, all that will remain of you will be a spoonful, barely enough to fill the cradle of my hands. The only end you'll bring about is your own. My boy!" she cried, and she laid her heavy head in my lap. The swelling heat and purity of her despair made my thinning soul lurch, but I could see no solution that would assuage both our hearts at once. "This performance, it will be your finale, can't you see, Limoges, *ma puce*? You expect me to idle on the ground beneath you as you take into your mouth the fatal morsel?"

I longed to tell Nathalie how fiercely I loved her, more even than I loved the absent moon, and I looked again in the mirror, cast my eyes upon my own disappearance. I said, "One last consumption, dear Nathalie. You must grant me a final farewell. Find for me the grandest sorrow you can spot in this crowd of hearts gnawed to tatters."

Nathalie rose wearily to her feet and said, "Very well, Limoges."

The full house was more restless than usual, the ringing dejection of the universe having reached such a pitch it was difficult to hear anything else. I looked out at the audience for Jonathan Albright's careworn face, but the bright lights washed out the particulars and left me seeing only intimations.

The other performers dragged themselves on and off stage with little enthusiasm, some of them already tottering with downed spirits. The stage manager himself looked vaguely pickled, as though he'd stumbled into a tub of brine, his cheeks damp and unnaturally ruddy.

I climbed the ladder and waited for the curtain to rise. As it did, the eye of the spotlight blinked and row upon row of suffering was revealed to me. I could manage to swallow only three sorrows a night, and every night we were full to the rafters with the world's grief, arms beseeching Nathalie to choose their hearts to lighten. It was now clear as glass to me that I could swallow for eternity and the abdomen of the world's unhappiness would remain just as distended as it always had been. Earthly despair was a gibbous moon forever waxing. In this moment I understood the sound that had erupted from that alienated anarchist just before he laid his hand, with a sense of irreversible sorrow, on the revolver.

I looked down for Nathalie and saw instead the stage manager tugging at a rope, an apoplectic glower further reddening his cheeks. The air in the theater was close and the audience shifted moodily like animals whip tamed and gravely expectant.

I looked up and could see that the moon and stars had not descended, and the stage manager was trying to dislodge them from heaven. Then I heard a windy "Oof!" explode from the stage manager, and the moon fell from the firmament, and from across the audience came a slowly rolling din of gasping as the spectators gazed upon it. The moon swung toward me, and I saw what it was that caused these stargazers to let go their grief long enough to exclaim over that of another: braided round the crescent sickle was Nathalie, limbs so intricately entwined with those of the moon that there'd be no extracting her, rope cinched at her throat—the fate of this wooden moon was now hers as well. The stage manager lost his grip on the hoist, and the half-silvered moon and my knotted Nathalie plummeted to the ground. With neither volition nor thought, I followed.

It was not the fall that broke the bottle inside me. I landed next to Nathalie, and hers was the last sorrow I drank. *In the light of the moon, Limoges, mon cher, lend me for a moment your capacious heart.* I put her hand to my lips and breathed as she traced with her fingers the words, *My boy, my own boy, my little moon, you must cease the consumption of the world's sorrow. There is no end to it.* She stroked my cheek. *I was once a supple and ignorant girl who swelled with child but continued to braid her body around the baby inside her, twisting herself into messages she hoped might make someone see her and love her, and this caused that baby to pack its bags, to flee the soup pot before it had finished stewing in the broth of her. But I was unable to give you up, my Limoges. You were always the lump of sugar in my tea.* My heart seized as I took inside me the scalding air of her sorrow, a deeply personal sadness, one born of love and remorse. This was the element of my healing that had always been wanting, had left me a sad gastronome with an appetite that knew no satiety: love, that which saps suffering of all abstraction. I looked in her eyes, partially eclipsed by the horn of the wooden moon, and understood at last that it was her, not the moon, from whom I had fallen.

When the bottle of sorrow inside me broke, my spirit's animating marrow rushed from me and infected the audience, who gave themselves over gratefully to its annihilating typhoon and have never been seen again.

The Funambules still perform on occasion, Marcel singing sweetly astride Guillaume, who clomps carefully across the stage in his boots. The stage manager divides his time between the cemetery and the sanatorium, where I lie inside an iron capsule. At all hours you'll find at one end of the hospital a pianist stroking the keys of a calliope, which whistles steam into tubes that are attached to the capsule and forcibly inflates my lungs, a pianist whom the stage manager spends his life savings to remunerate.

Sometimes the stage manager sings to me at night as he sits beside me, songs of thwarted love and lilacs, starving sailors and dying candles. He gazes at me through a window in the lung, and I imagine I know what the moon feels when its disciples look up toward its illumination with weary longing. "Rest now, Limoges," he says, his face pressed against the glass. "You work too hard, dear boy." He tap-taps to the rhythm of the music filling my chamber, tap-taps, perhaps waiting for me to hatch.

Moon, Moon, My Honey

My husband was in charge of the Nightly Improbable Joke, broadcast punctually every evening at 10:05 p.m., the world's appetite for improbability peaking, he calculated, just before bedtime. One night he said, "How many polar bears does it take to light up the moon?" And I said, "Polar bears?" I said, "Moon?" He waited a second until he was sure everyone in the listening audience had mulled it over and come up wanting. He was known for his timing. "None," he said, "because the sky over the tundra cannot bear such thickly insulated illumination lest the ice caps dissolve and return us all to the sea." And then he added, "*Ursus maritimus.*" He covered his mouth to cork a chortle, and I smiled at him. Blankly but sincerely. "Glub," he whispered, and he touched my lips. Then there was a moment for silent cogitation, and I could feel heads nodding quizzically inside the lit-up houses that shone beyond the radio tower in the blue-black night. We left the studio and went to our drafty home, and I lay down and curled against him and dreamt of bears lumbering down the winter boulevard in luxurious electric coats that sometimes spelled out words in tiny light bulbs: *honeymoon, tumor, desolation, lunatic.*

Now that my husband is gone, all the jokes are a good deal more probable and the townspeople, who'd been more reliant upon my husband's thoughtfully implausible humor than they'd realized, seem vague, vitamin deficient, a look of postponement graying their faces.

Q: How many grieving hearts does it take to light up the moon?

"Buried treasure is only useful so long as it stays buried," my husband once told me. I blinked at him philosophically. "Hope must be suspended to be sustained." Blink. "It's fruition that causes hope to wither. And what do we have without it? A longing fulfilled? No future in that." He'd been peeling potatoes all morning with a kind of grim efficiency. He'd slept fitfully the night before. He turned to me, and his face was limned in a stammering incandescence. He had a beautiful smile that spread across his face like a concertina opening.

A: The moon is a greedy guts, with a rapacious appetite exactly the size of itself. But there's a hole in the bottom that leaks stardust, spills it across the midnight sky, and the moon, drained of light, begins to fade, doomed to hunger, insatiable. Every night it must eat again.

A: The moon will swallow every barely beating heart it finds washed up on shore. Some nights you can see scattered everywhere a spongy pale pinkness pulsating amidst the pebbles, those deceptive pebbles that wink at night like a million doubloons just waiting to fill your pockets.

I had always lived near the sea, which frequently vomits onto shore things that irritate its briny guts.

I was one of those things.

That night, the man who would become my husband click-clickety-clicked along the shore with his metal detector and stumbled upon me, then freed me from the tight bandage of weeds in which the sea had swaddled me. He pressed the water from my chest, and I spit fish onto the sand and sputtered to life. The exhaled fish sizzled and flopped toward the ragged tide. He said I looked like an eggplant he'd once raised, so perfectly bulbous and purple beneath its green zucchetto that he hadn't had the heart to eat it. I told him I thought I'd been bobbing for a while and was likely not at my most attractive. He said, "Au contraire," and though it wasn't entirely clear to me what he meant by this, I could see he smiled without irony. I plucked the algae from my hair. I watched his mouth retain a friendly shape and agreed it can be difficult to eat things that have come to be purple on their own. His was not the first mind that the thought of making a meal of me had crossed. The sea belched behind us.

I asked him to please help me find Sprocket, my dog. He too was cocooned in seaweed, and he coughed up whiskered fish when we pressed on his belly. He remained lying on his side, eyes closed, then his tail scraped the sand like a windshield wiper. The man smiled and chucked Sprocket under the muzzle. There was always a pleasing geometry to Sprocket's movements, and I found I liked having someone to share this with. "Seadog," said the man, and it was true, at that moment a white rainbow shimmered mistily in the distance, the ocean's weary exhalation visible in the chill of twilight.

"Where did you come from?" asked the man who would one day be my husband. I shook my head, I looked at the sky, I looked at the sea. Sprocket licked my hand. He wobbled and stood, uncertainly, as though unaccustomed to being four legged. The fur around his muzzle was matted in stringy clumps, making him appear to sport a Fu Manchu. He looked like he was about to make a sage prediction in a language I could not speak. I scratched his long nose and he shook off the sea.

The man gave me his hand and pulled me to my feet. "I'm so glad you found me," he said.

He said his name was Mahoney Mahoney and that he went by his last name. "Mahoney?" I said. He shook his head. "Mahoney," I said. He nodded. I felt my scalp pulsing. Mahoney pulled a minnow from behind my ear and handed it to me like a maritime magician.

A: The moon is a bottomless pelican no boatload of minnows will ever satisfy.

Mahoney took me to his house and lent me some dungarees. He made carrot soup and offered the greens to a mouse, who trotted confidently across the floor and stood at his feet as he stirred. I could see this mouse was no stranger to this arrangement, and somehow this made me feel minute and momentary, as though I'd fallen a phylum or two, in the direction of Amoebozoa. Sprocket lay across the welcome mat, and the mouse tugged its spoils in front of his nose, stopped and stared confrontationally. The mouse exuded a certain confidence and aimed at him a festering look, like it could raise its paw and topple a tiny empire. Sprocket opened his eyes, his head still resting on his paws, shifting his gaze in one direction and then the other, his eyebrows bouncing noncommittally, then he sighed through his nose and went back to sleep. All night I could hear the mouse dragging top after top across the floor, and eventually there was a great din of nibbling.

As I lay upon the sofa in front of the quieting crackle of the fireplace, I thought about the sea life that had wriggled around me—in the ocean you cannot get lonely, which is one of the disquieting things about the ocean—and I wondered if I'd ever feel dry again. I could imagine eating more soup with this man and thought I might grow accustomed to this mouse and its entitlements in time.

A: There's not enough light in the universe to feed the moon's blinding bloat.

They gave my husband to me in a small velvet bag. "You've made a mistake," I said. "My husband was 6'2", taller when he stood on his toes, which he often did. He had the shapely calves of a person who longed to be stratospheric. The woman at the crematorium wore a hairnet and an apron, and I wondered if she also worked at the school cafeteria. She hugged me and walked away.

There are those widows who will not open letters or closets or crack open picture albums, who sit in their houses carefully not looking at things, their eyes trained on that one spot in the far corner of the kitchen they know their husbands never stepped foot on, but I am of the other sort. I opened the bag immediately, and what I saw inside were those pebbles that blink yearningly in the moonlight.

A: The moon makes handsome detritus of us all.

Here I am again, sodden as seaweed, marooned on the desert island of my despair.

Mahoney told me a story about sea sisters named Creeping Jeebies, Boof Alarum, and Bugaboo, who shared one eye and two teeth. *They had the bodies of swans and the hairless heads and withered arms of beautiful primordial crones, and even without teeth they were argumentative, as swans and crones are known to be. They were so old, they were contemporaries of the moon, whom they had known in the moon's childhood, though they had never been children or cygnets themselves. After many years of paddling across the ocean with their waxy black feet, snatching harpoons from the air in their toothless maws just before the razor points sank into the hearts of whales, and slowly gnawing holes in the hulls of ships, their teeth developed caries, and their eye, overworked and too often exposed to the elements, grew milky with a coming blindness. They knew if they could part the curtain of membrane with one of their crumbling teeth, they could see the world in all its objectionable clarity again and find their favorite rock in the sea, the one they liked to lie on in the moonlight while the sea spray salted their feathered bellies. They'd drifted away from it many years ago while trailing a whaler and had been searching for it with their dimming vision ever since. "I think it's yonder," said Bugaboo, pointing indeterminately. "Give me that thing," growled Boof Alarum, and she seized the eye, popped it in her head, and looked through the gauze for home, but all she could see were faraway dolphins stitching the waves.*

Creeping Jeebies cradled the eye in the crook of her arm and cooed to it, but she couldn't figure a way to operate on the eye without the surgical guidance of the eye. Just then a swordfish sawed through the waves, and Creeping Jeebies plucked it from the water by the crescent moon of its dorsal fin and hoisted it into the air.

"You must help us remove the blindness!" honked Boof Alarum. "We are lost, we are LOST!"

"The ocean is everywhere," said the swordfish. Boof Alarum opened her mouth as if to scream, but the sound, too frightened to depart the comfortable confines of her lungs, fizzled inside her. "Of

course to be everywhere," said the swordfish, "is also to be nowhere,"
and it flipped its tail emphatically.

Bugaboo whinnied, "Nobody likes a philosophical swordfish."

"Root hog or die!" bleated Boof Alarum.

"En garde!" shrieked the swordfish, and it sliced the film from
the eye and leapt out of the hag's gnarled clutches.

Then Creeping Jeebies began to weep and hiccup, for when the
scrim fell from their sight, she saw their beloved rock rise up before
her; she saw the stymied harpoons piled up around it: they'd been
swimming in a circle for years, around and around their heart's fond-
est longing. "Which is," said the man who would become my husband, "so often the case."

As night fell onto the water, Creeping Jeebies grabbed her sisters
by their tail feathers and tugged them onto the rock, now whittled
by time and the corrosive tides to no bigger than a minute. And the
moon shone on the glinting eggs of their fetching heads, which they
tucked into their feathered backs, their one eye rolling from socket
to socket to enable the sisters' dreaming.

Mahoney dropped a crust to the floor, and the mouse toddled
in, twitched its whiskers in my direction, and toddled out again.
Sprocket moved his head from one paw to the other.

We sat in front of the hearth, and Mahoney warmed my ears
with his hands. I said, "Who am I in that story?" and he answered,
"You are the ocean." He stoked the fire and held my feet until I fell
asleep.

Mahoney did improbable stand-up in clubs that served only salad
and beer. It was widely believed that greens prepare a body to be
entertained. He said, "Good evening, ladles and gramophones." The
people in the audience nodded their heads and sometimes ap-
plauded, though they were not prone to smiling. Proximity to the
sea made outward signs of jollity impractical. The water was always
gnashing its waves at the landed, and no one wanted to be its patsy.
Sometimes he talked about me, his wife, whom the ocean, in a moment of intemperate generosity, had gifted him. There were people
in the audience who looked at their mates longingly and imagined

them bedecked in clamshells and coral and a garland of algae. Everyone knew our story, and it made the town hopeful. Sometimes they left appreciative pebbles and tins of sardines at our table.

My husband told me, "Everywhere, somebody believes something, and sometimes it might be true."

Mahoney told me the moon was magnetic. He said the water was the north-seeking pole, the moon the south, and that on the night of our meeting the moon had tugged the tides toward shore and delivered me to him. Or him to me. For years he'd stood at his kitchen window with the mouse, stirring and stirring, parceling peelings, waiting and mooning for he knew not what. And then he saw the moon flash and the sea glint, and he took to the beach with his metal detector in search of any oscillation in the magnetic field. He found two spoons, a nail file, a golf shoe, and me.

In his kitchen there was a wooden display case, on whose rungs miniature spoons dangled, souvenir spoons from various stars he pointed out to me in the sky: Sirius, Canopus, Denebola, Zubenelgenubi.

Alone with Sprocket and the mouse in the kitchen, I looked at the constellation of his fingerprints on the window, tracing the radial loops with my eyes, those cresting swells that had once touched me. I laid my face against the smudges: *Pollux, Aldebaran, Betelgeuse, Iota Draconis.*

In those undulating days before Mahoney left me, he seemed to float away from us, grow remote, like a destination in a dream. The nearer I came to him, the farther away he was: at the window, down the beach, beneath the radio tower, on the moon. His skin turned both pale and vaguely violet, like milk in which blueberries have been allowed to stew, and his mouth grew increasingly hard to find. On the night before Mahoney left me for good, we sat on the beach where he'd first discovered me, mummied in vegetation, and watched the light tinsel the waves and lap at our feet. Sprocket lay with his head draped heavily across Mahoney's lap, an adoring anvil. My husband had been quiet that day, and I saw in his face what I later realized was the sadness of hope's return.

He scratched Sprocket's head, and I took his other hand in mine. I pressed his fingers and imagined a lunar music that could be apprehended only by touch. I said, "How many Mahoneys does it take to send me over the moon?" and I smiled recklessly. He opened his mouth to speak but didn't. I looked at his front teeth, which overlapped as if huddling for warmth. Everything about him was deeply hospitable and endeared me to a world I'd once resolved to have no part of. I'll go whither those teeth goest, I thought. At that moment, every atom of me aligned in such a way as to make the matter of me ecstatically disappear, visible only from the summit of space.

He lay down, and we gathered around him like a storm in search of an eye. He said if we pressed against him, the vital fluid of our collective magnetism would pool inside him, "best communicated," he whispered to me so that Sprocket and the mouse would not hear, "by the thumbs." He was considerate that way. He said we'd be able to see through his body as through an aquarium and could find those dark and deadly fish swimming inside him, could pluck the needle-toothed gluttons from his belly and throw them into the sea, which was better equipped to deal with such villainy.

That night, the new moon shone invisibly behind us and the mouse gazed hopefully in its direction, as if waiting for the next shaving of rind to fall upon its busy nose. A mouse is nothing if not optimistic. The mouse pressed its paws against Mahoney's cheek, Sprocket laid his head across his belly, and I placed my hands on his chest. Mahoney's body shook like a strait gripped by squall, and we watched as his flesh took on a murky glow, as if licked by the dim light of a guttering candle. We held tight as his insides churned, but, as I pushed my hands deeper into the brackish infirmity, the life inside him swam through my grasp, and I could see we were powerless to repel the marine magnetism pulling him under.

The afternoon before he died, he told me everything he knew he owed to me, and I understood he meant I was the proof of his beliefs, proof of the famished moon, the darkly bountiful sea, proof of animal and electromagnetism, I was the outcome of a hypnotic longing. His was a heart as pure and vulnerable as that one oyster that secretes its pearl only in the absence of a shell, the one that re-fuses to be protected. What he proved to me is that the one thing worth the risk of drowning is love.

When I left the house, Sprocket and the mouse sat watching at the window. The mouse flapped its tail, and I could see it was regretful. Sprocket bellowed quietly and shifted from foot to foot.

Nights, I had used Mahoney's metal detector and gone sniffing down the dunes. Over the weeks, I amassed a great horde: horse-shoes and penny nails and cookie tins and wedding rings and bottle caps and money clips and button hooks and candle dampers and ice picks and watch fobs and hair combs and toy soldiers and belt buck-les and bedsprings and enough spoons to keep soup moving from every bowl to every mouth for all eternity. The spoons I soldered together to make a suit.

Mahoney told me that this place where we live is the center of gravity, the nadir of buoyancy, the point at which a body is most leaden, so it has taken me a long time to collect enough spoons to catch the moon's eye. But the moon is a ravenous raven and can be bought with a sizeable glint.

The radio tower was orange and pierced those clouds that tall and narrow things always attract. I clanked as I scaled it and carried round my wrist the velvet bag of my husband. I'd made this trip many times before, and it had taken me some hours to reach the top under less freighted conditions. I timed it so that I'd reach the tower's peak by nightfall. I'd heard once of a man who made a suit of ducks and leapt from a lofty bluff, but ducks are not easily mag-netized and so would not likely get a person far beyond a familiar atmosphere. No, my destiny rested in the magnetic ambitions of spoons.

Q: *How many spoons does it take to ferry a broken heart to the moon, and will my husband be there to greet me?*

As the sky turned a shiny black, I reached the zenith. Now that there were no more improbable jokes to hear, the tower no longer crackled with transmission. Here I had spent the last months fashioning a catapult, a spoon the size of my body, and I settled my heavily be-spooned body in the bowl. I stared up into the illumination of my final destination, the last time my neck would hold such an angle. I cut the rope.

As I sailed through the air, I remembered, fondly, what it had felt like to breathe water. With each passing inch, I felt the moon's potent pull, its tidal attraction, felt it tugging my suit, my body, swiftly into its orbit. My heart fluttered as the earth grew round beneath me, as the moon's molten surface flattened before me. I thought about what I might find on arrival. Maybe I'd miscalculated, was one spoon shy of delivery, and would bobble eternally among the stars. Maybe the moon, so smitten with my suit, might not give me up, might clutch me to its breast and press me flat. Perhaps widows roamed the shores of the moon's oceans, emptying their velvet bags upon the pebbles, a riprap of grief.

And now here I am, afloat again in my trek toward love or annihilation, the only two choices we have.

Over these years I've spent voyaging through the magnetosphere and beyond, my hair has grown long and liquid, streaming behind me like quicksilver, furling in the wake of my own astrophysics. The air here is very agreeable and lends my skin an implausible sheen my honey, Mahoney, will like. It calls to mind that carrot soup. Some nights the moon disappears, and I fear that I've overshot it or gone blind while I slept. I worry the magnetic fields will grow impatient, cancel my heart's errand, and toss me back to the sea. I plan to make amends with the omnivorous moon, whom I once thought ill of, the minute I clap eyes on my husband. As I rocket through the atmosphere, I let hope swim inside me, and I clutch my husband tightly in my hand.

GOD

Threnody

The Dead, those practical jokers, are never dead for long. After they've lain in the grave or urn or crypt for three days, they rise, like bread, warm and fermented, revive as if from a delicious but vaguely disturbing sleep, a sleep deep, deep, and riddled with dream, and they shake out their limbless limbs, reassemble the sodden flesh, and move moodily about, famished wildcats. They remember everything about their deaths, the sputter of breath, the wavering faces crowded above them, which makes them a little cross, as you might imagine. It is not nearly as reassuring to awaken into the airless atmosphere of an afterlife as they'd hoped.

The Prophets are the slowest to rouse. For all their sure-footed divinations, they are the most likely to have nursed a scrap of doubt, which occasionally expressed itself in Life as a dull throb in the optic nerve. Their eyes would water with uncertainty, and they'd fall to their knees and sleep. In Death, they unwrap themselves, like a gift, unfurl their beards, which grew at a hastened pace when their hearts ceased to beat, and try to conceal their disappointment. They know better than anyone the spring-loaded trap of expectation, its jagged jaws. They pride themselves on being able to make do; they can defer desire eternally, even without the cautionary overindulgence of the Wicked to guide them. *It will come, it will come, it will come,* they have murmured, *one day.* . . . Their shoulders are ropy beneath their robes from having borne the onus of revelation. They squint in the new light and are well pleased to feel the ache in their bellies that is an absence of hunger.

It is the Murderers, of course, who make a racket, loud enough to wake the . . . wait, thinks one. Where am I? He eyes warily the do-gooder milksops around him. This is no place for an assassin! He roars and imagines leg irons, which he rattles vigorously. The Prophets do not bat an eye. He sidles up stealthily—he knows how to appear suddenly at the victim's back, inside his unsuspecting shadow, as if out of nowhere, trick of the trade—and gives the Prophets his most menacing glower, daggers speeding from his eyes to their hearts. Prophets, however, do not startle easily. They look at him forbearingly, and he feels the top of his scalp prickle with exasperation. He pulls a switchblade from inside his boot, snaps it open, carves an S in the air, and holds it to a Prophet's insubstantial throat. Nothing, not a shudder, not a gasp, no begging, no tears. The Prophet's eyes are round with forgiveness. The Murderer feels ineffectual. He slumps on a rock and picks his teeth.

The Innocent feel they've been misled. Did they shield themselves from Knowledge for nothing? Where is the reward for never falling, remaining upright and ignorant, if they've cast their lot with Murderers and Prophets? These blue-eyed Marys, they become sullen and sigh loudly, the sound of innocence evacuating. Innocence lost, they begin to torment the Prophets with sharpened sticks, poke them in the ear, the navel, the buttocks, never drawing blood, of course, and they jeer at the Murderers from a healthy distance.

The Intellectuals are perfectly devastated. It never occurred to them that . . . well, all of it. Resurrection?! Ugh. That was not an idea that *ever* appealed to them, not for a second. When they think of the existential conundrums they fed themselves on, the well-basted speculations that were their meat and drink, now sham nourishment, they could just kill themselves all over again. They sit, hug their stork legs, hang prominent chins between their knees, self-spitefully refuse to clean the oily smudge from their spectacles, tie and untie their wingtips, and abandon themselves to unoriginal thoughts. *Dark, dark day*, they mumble as they survey the flat and weatherless landscape that is their . . . fate (they wince), *empty words, alas, only signs*, and this thought seeds a reluctant smile. *Here, in this* (they scratch their worn-out noddles thoughtfully), *this, this*

arid, sterile (they cast their gaze toward what once was the indifferent sky, rub their jaws meaningfully) *no man's land of no represen-
tation . . . endless space . . . liberated,* they think, it comes to them
suddenly, *yes! liberated of interpretation, so far beyond multivalence
we arrive at last at the singular, the essential, the aboriginal Logos!*
their hearts seize, *the Final Discourse, hegemony of hegemonies,
where we lope wordlessly about* (they stand and pace, their unkempt
hair waving frantically about their heads like incandescence),
*hermeneutically bereft in this desolate wasteland of ineluctable, in-
expressible perfection!* No one listens, not a soul, and the familiarity
of this lends them a narcotic comfort, and they nap.

And then there are the Monkeys, everywhere, resentful and
drowsy, fed up with infinite theorems and the pressure to turn
xlkc#jvie8&5ish into *Hamlet* or *Henry* or *All's Well That Ends
Well*—what monkey these days has *that* sort of time on his hands,
they'd like to know—awaiting evolution, as they have for millennia,
drumming opposable thumbs on their hairy knees, promises, promises, sprawled on every rock, too weary to pick a nit: a mystery even
to God.

They All miss the passing of Time, which once slipped from the
body like gas, a malodorous relief.

When God finally appears to the Dead, after they've wandered
about in the hilly nothingness that is their unrelenting future, hoping
to discern a hostile climate—hailstorms, arctic winds, hurricanes,
anything against which they must shelter themselves—He takes
the form of an egg, hardboiled, and they tap His shell with their
shoes. They tap-tap gingerly at first, then single mindedly, like min-
ers who have finally uncovered a vein of gold, peel the shell away,
and bore through the rubbery white until the yoke, that ylem of
God, blinds them and they raise their arms gratefully. The sound
they make as they stagger about in the broken remains is a crackling
hosanna. *Praise God, prays God, preys God,* crunch, crunch . . .
crunch crunch crunch.

If only they could see the look of boredom that makes the yoke
crumble with despair. **Ideals, ideals, oh spare me the ideals!** thinks
God. **Where's the calumny, the malice, the gluttonous greed?** It's

true, the thick wool of iniquity is forever shorn from the pink and risen soul once these pardoned sheep get a load of the Almighty, their truculent shepherd. **Day in, day out, is there no end,** He wonders, **to My irrelevance (which is,** He thinks, **the same as being the Be-All and End-All, Alpha and Omega, Long and Short of It, that is to say: Null and Void)?** *Praise Cod!* warbles God, that prickly pear, a mocking sneer crimping His imagined mouth, fish lips flapping, His infinite mind leaden with brooding, smoldering with grief. Each day He visits the Dead, they nearly shatter His heart. He has long fantasized about bringing Eternity to a shuddering halt: ONCE. AND. FOR. ALL. Ohhhhhh. He's not sure how much longer He can bear it.

Now the atmosphere is teeming with God, the churlish mope, and He gathers the diaphanous ooze and flutter of Himself into His infinite arms like a voluminous laundress collecting the soiled linens and shirtfronts and trousers and kerchiefs of the world. An impossible task, that's what God is, He won't deny it.

Meanwhile, the Dead dance, blind as moles! They wait, they wait, pointlessly they wait, for Time they wait, they wait for Time to pass.

In the Hatred of a Minute

When Time was a little girl, she couldn't wait to grow up. At four, no stranger to blood, she got her period. At six, she married a train conductor. Nobody ever loved her so well as the train conductor. Except perhaps the country of Switzerland. History, who walked around with warheads and that inaugural wheel and fightin' words and a triceratops or two and the Golden Horde and creation myths featuring a landscape cobbled together from the hips and breasts and randomly strewn extremities of a savaged body and the Big Bang and bombardiers and bad decisions and Stonehenge and the Flat Earth, and its dead partisans, and the Vin Fiz Flyer and blazing villages and Marie Antoinette and multiple paradigm shifts and the Bronze Age and Aramaic and slave ships and the telltale iridium layer blanketing the bones of dinosaurs and the pathological insecurities of despots all falling from his mouth, had mixed feelings about her. He depended on her but sometimes thought of her as his bitch. Unlike the train conductor, he was impossible to kiss. He liked facts more than theories, men more than women, war more than peace, the victor more than the vanquished, carrots more than parsnips, and had not been a good father to Historicity and Historiography, latchkey offspring who raised themselves from a tender age. History does not like to think of himself as a nightmare from which a famous fictional character cannot awake. Writers are all such Gloomy Gusses, thinks History, they should just leave him out of it, honestly. History, History feels compelled to point out, never did anything without the will and sanction of nettled men.

But Time, she's always passing, dying 86,400 deaths a day. Time hasn't time enough for fear or grief. Or knitting. Or long walks along the beach. Woodworking. Kickboxing. She once tried tai chi, but it made her anxious. As does the soothing music piped into the waiting rooms of dentists; she could grind her crowns to dust listening to that. Time wears a cardigan so as not to freeze. Time has always wanted to travel to the moon, in a sleeping berth, rocked to sleep by the rhythmic wobble of the rocket. In the absence of gravity, her bones and purpose would thin and she'd become more mollusk than sundown, more inchworm than equinox. She'll make that possible one day, discount travel to other planets. *In Time are all things possible,* Time's mother used to tell her after Time came home from a long, hard day of being heckled by those geniuses she went to John Dewey Junior High with: *Time passes,* they crowed as she walked by, *just like gas!* That had made her persona non grata in the cafeteria. Time's mother told her just to take it a day at a time, things were bound to improve, junior high would not last forever. Time shuddered at the thought.

Though she received the usual training, Time does not understand the concept of light years or the evolution and high octane death of stars, does not understand how she might only be gazing at a memory, at a history, when she looks at the light-spangled sky, at a long-dead brightness, seeing the star as it was a thousand years ago. No, she does not understand how it can be true that she's staring at deaths that have not yet caught up with the dying, slow-as-molasses extinctions that have not yet reached the eyes of the beholder, thermonuclear reactions she authorized years ago. Time looks at the sky throbbing with light and makes herself think, *That star is ten light years away, and though it's now an adult, what I'm witnessing is its childhood.* All those dead children hanging in the sky. Who can bear to exist in the face of that? Time stops thinking. For Time, things happen when they happen. And things are always happening. Time's dance card is always full.

Time's sister, Emily, was recently diagnosed with a fatal illness that will cause her body to fail organ by organ. There will be a cure for this disease in the future, some years after Emily, at the age of sixteen, will have died.

Time imagines looking in the sky and seeing eight-year-old Emily chasing the other perishing stars with a butterfly net.

A famous man, friend of History's (they can be so terribly dull, though this one harbored a boyhood tenderness for silver foxes and loved to twinkle on the tips of his hammertoes in an imagined pas de deux when alone in his bedchamber), once said that Time was God's way of preventing all things from occurring at once, and this made her feel purposeful, even if she could ill afford to be a disciple of someone who nourishes himself thin as a slip on timelessness. She and God have gone round on this point before, when she has urged him to imagine an ending, a grand finale, a way out, an omega. *Just think about it*, she says slyly (for God, thinking is as good as doing). He doesn't seem happy with the way things are going anyway, always brooding, talk about a Gloomy Gus. History will continue to bluster about God even after he's gone. God would become glamorous in death, a source of wistful longing, imagine the teary obituaries, the memorial cook-offs, there would be protests and rallies to resuscitate him, people would plant lilies in formerly sacred places, instead of setting themselves and others ablaze, wouldn't that be nice for a change? Time was all about change. There was a time when God was thought to be dead, before his penumbra was sighted hovering over Bucksnort, Alabama. Time has pointed out to God that she is meat and milk of many religions. Without her there could be no Second Coming, no Ancient of Days, no day of Brahma, no Dreamtime, no eternity, no spinning Kalachakra, and certainly no apocalypse or End Times with which to harrow the brethren. God is careful not to look Time in the face, for if he did he might be fixed in place on the spot, and then where would he be? And when? Time sometimes whispers in his ear as he casts a remorseful gaze across the clear-cut forest of the future, old growth felled and gone, *Your Time has come.*

God tries to imagine what would happen to the universe were he no longer its custodian, its bricoleur, its brawny doorman, its stenographer, documentarian, midwife, wet nurse, internist-alienist-mesmerist-iridologist, its sniper, its puppeteer. Would it be better off? He's made some mistakes. Not intervening in suffering, for example, as though he were just a naturalist tracking a pride of starving lions, one who felt it was his duty to remain at an impartial distance and let nature do what nature does, which is eat things, so when that baby elephant comes along, frantically searching for its herd after a sandstorm, all he can do is close his eyes and keep the camera rolling. Yes, that was one rule he regretted. But he doesn't think it's hubris to believe that without him all motion would screech to a halt, all mass would begin to transmogrify and come to resemble the diaphanous and hesitant radiance that is the Creator, and this might not be such a desirable thing; to be cast in his image is to see a ravenous absence when you walk by a mirror. One theologian-turned-agnostic called God (a little spitefully, he thought, no need to resort to name calling, nothing more scornful than a convert to disbelief) a pandemic, and God began to see himself this way too, and sometimes he wished there were a vaccine, but these are thoughts God indulges only once every billion years—why should he listen to humans, those misanthropic toddlers of the universe?—and then he tucks them away in the deepest, most bottomless recesses of his unconscious (what those meddlesome string theorists are always trying to lasso), and now he bats Time aside, which causes her to reel, and in that moment, in *that* moment, *this* moment, every sleeping creature dreams of an orphaned mitten and an empty bottle sitting atop a mountain inhabited only by a dying glacier, but then Time settles and she tends to the day, her overgrown garden; she weeds the minutes and tills the hours. *Your Time has come and gone,* she whispers to herself. And then the dreamers wake with only a faint residue of the abjection of having been abandoned by Time, and they slap walls as they walk and drink glass upon glass of water.

When Time and Emily were children, they played the misfortune and torture game. *Would you rather be born without feet or constantly sneeze glass, a bloody handkerchief always falling from your pocket?* asked Emily. Time had a thing about the questionable hygiene of handkerchiefs, as Emily well knew, so the choice was an easy one. And in fact footlessness, she thought, might be useful in slowing a girl down. She'd been accused of lolloping more than once. *Would you rather kill everyone you've ever known and loved or be the salve the wounded apply to their weeping sores?* asked Time, and Emily looked at her mournfully and laid her tiny hand upon her shoulder.

Time is everyone's favorite assassin.

Time learned to drive and received her learner's permit when she was eight, and she careened about recklessly as if there were no tomorrow, a dream she sometimes had. But there was and she woke to see snow covering the family Corvair like a winter pelt. It made Time long for a durable pet, maybe a Galápagos tortoise, a loud-mouthed macaw, something that could at least see her through to the next century, if not the one after that. That morning she did poorly on her algebra quiz. Sometimes Time failed math on principle.

Time feels abstract, her heart flutters. She cannot see her knees.

By the time Time was 4.5 billion years old, she'd seen some things, things that made even God turn the sound down. She watched as human beings, those Johnny-come-latelies, ate everything around them, leaving behind dental impressions on every extinction. Time was born with a stubborn nostalgia, and she missed the dodo even before it squawked and stumbled gracelessly in and out of existence.

Once Time went to her in-laws' house for Easter dinner, and she ate only scalloped potatoes and Parker House rolls. The train conductor's mother sniffed accusingly and intimated that Time had been packing it on lately and would be wise to watch her figure, go easy on the starch. She made a joke about the fullness of Time. The train conductor's mother was no will-o'-the-wisp herself, but Time kept her trap shut. She spooned four wizened peas onto her plate. Then the train conductor's mother told Time she had an all-natural cream with aloe and almond oil that might help deflate the bags beneath her eyes. Time had not slept since she was three years old. Preparing eternally for the future can keep a girl from getting the proper shut-eye, but there was no explaining this to the train conductor's mother, who was not a career woman and who slept like a truckload of lead and snored like a jackhammer. "Your eyes look like they're packed and ready for a long trip!" hooted her husband's mother. Time swallowed a pea and told her mother-in-law the date and hour of her death, and her mother-in-law spent the rest of the meal dabbing spittle from the corner of her mouth and absently plucking cloves from the ham's glazed backside.

Later, Time would feel regretful and make her mother-in-law forget, though she'd retain a persistent and nagging unease in the presence of Time and would always sit with her back to the wall.

Contrary to popular belief, Time, a fretful traveler, never flies, but she does enjoy walking. She believes it impolite to arrive at a destination too quickly. Sometimes even bicycling gives her the bends.

When her husband comes home at night, after an arduous day of conducting, he likes Time to stop and throw her arms about his neck. In this glistering second: _ _ nobody dies. Bodies accumulate like corncobs at a picnic. The universe explodes with excessive human occupancy every day at 6:00 p.m. sharp.

At 6:01, the world suffers anew.

When Time was thirty-eight, she burned her hand on a waffle iron, and now her lifeline looks like it's incarcerated, and it makes her miss her father, who made burnt waffles for her and her sister once while on weekend furlough, the only bread they ever broke together. Time heals slowly, so slowly, more slowly than you might imagine.

Truth is, Time and God dated for a short time when Time was in college. She never told the train conductor about this as he already suffers from feelings of inadequacy, and he needs to be alert at work, not measuring himself against impossible standards for heaven's sake. This was when Time was a contortionist, mostly on weekends, bendable as a whip of licorice, how she put herself through school. Budding physicists paid good money to watch Time bend, watch her gyrate behind glass or dance on their laps. They tried to coax her to talk about how she started, how a nice girl like her, and sometimes she told them a story, both true and not, as all stories are, about a broken home, father in and out of the slammer, a mother who worked double shifts at the cog-and-fob factory, and a little brother with a mysterious illness, who could never go out in the sun, who played alone in moonlight as other children's eyes quivered with dreams. The physicists sobbed as they dandled Time on their knees and stroked her silken cheeks, tried to think of a way they could save her from this sordid life, deliver her from these unfortunate circumstances. And then the curtain fell.

One of the many problems that doomed Time's romance with God was that he was never on time, and no amount of couples counseling (to which he invariably arrived late and full of breathless excuses—he made it clear he just wasn't comfortable talking about their problems with a stranger; oh, and that was another problem, God's passive aggression—the Old Testament days of God, then in his adolescence, blowing his stack and drowning the universe at the faintest aggravation, those days were long gone, and though Time was grateful for this, weary as she was of starting over and over and over again, still she wished he'd learn to express his anger more directly and to compartmentalize less; that, she thought, had begun with enumerating the deadly sins, between which Time thought there was a *lot* of overlap, whether God saw it or not, gluttony, for example, just another species of lust, *Am I right?* she asked the therapist), no amount of therapy, would ever make God punctual (just ask those mopey sad-sack Millenarians).

God complained that he could hear Time ticking at night, like a bomb set to detonate upon sunrise, and it kept him more awake than usual, doubly omniscient, when what he really craved was a little ignorance, a little amnesia, so he stopped staying over.

Time, at her most lithe and flexible, *supple as string*, the physicists had said admiringly, used to lie awake at night worrying about the paradox of time travel and autoinfanticide—what if she traveled back in time and killed herself? (Many braggarts had claimed to kill Time, had claimed to waste her—she was forever getting death threats—but here she was still kicking, no bucket in sight, the sun going up, the sun going down . . .) And then that would mean that she would never have existed, which would mean she never traveled back in time in the first place, indeed there'd be no time in which to travel had Time been aborted in the womb, so, erm . . . Wait. A. Minute. It was at this moment that all sleeping people dreamt of the maudlin faces of handless clocks and woke up feeling so fatigued they realized it was actually the day before yesterday, and took a slug of Nyquil, so they could make it through the night to reach tomorrow one more time, eyeteeth and pie-in-the-sky aspirations more or less intact.

God tried to explain to Time the Novikov self-consistency principle, but there was such an air of superiority in his tone as he maundered on and on about *many worlds* and *quantum suicide* and the mortality of cats kept in the malevolent boxes of theorists and a man who becomes immortal shooting himself again and again with a loaded gun that refuses to fire la-la-la that she set the phone down and scrambled some eggs. She did the dishes, made a grocery list, cleaned out the crumb tray of her toaster, and picked up the phone again in time to hear God say, "Will I see you later?"

In the hospital room, Emily is surrounded by wheezing machinery and the usual life-sustaining drips, and she tells Time that she understands now what it means to be alone, but sometimes she imagines the tubes are tunnels through which a tiny civilization passes in and out of her body on their way to and from their jobs, the opera, the bank, their homes, each twinge of pain a pileup on the highway that leads to a failing interior, a torture she remembers from long ago, and then she understands that it is she who is lying in a room that dwells in the body of another, and she feels suddenly molecular and weightless, as though her skin were turning to starlight, and she is less afraid.

It's not that Time can't cry; it's that she's crying all the time, but nobody sees it. Her sorrow, the sad set of her mouth, the smudge of despair beneath her eyes, are invisible to others, announcing as they do the coming of loss, and loss, and loss, and that's her misfortune, her Cassandra Torture. Time says, "You'll always have me, Em," and Emily touches the place on Time's chin from where the invisible tears drop and says, "That's just what I don't have," and her mouth tries to smile.

On God and Time's first date, they went to a slasher film, God's choice, and God gasped five seconds before every out-of-nowhere chop of the ax. A man sitting in front of them turned around and glowered at God, who smiled apologetically, and then, midway through the movie, the man made a show of springing from his seat, throwing a snarl behind him, and stomping up the aisle. "Agnostic," God whispered to Time and shrugged.

When Time told God she thought it was better if they were just friends, God called her a cruel mistress. God knows, God was used to rejection, but he'd expected more from Time. He whinnied like a horse and balled his hands into fists, the floor began to tremble, objects hopped off shelves, and then the gathering squall in his eyes passed, and he promised to work on his shortcomings (or long-comings, whichever were more irksome, he'd change, he promised), but Time said she didn't want to change him and that she knew there were plenty of people in the world who loved God just the way he was, warts and all. God sighed so windily that Time fell backward, and all of a sudden there was Abraham Lincoln, whose drawn face looked like molten tallow, and Marie Curie, blinking amidst the glow that trailed her, there they were standing in the room between God and Time, looking a little shopworn and dispossessed. History, who hated it when someone speculated what Genghis Kahn and Mary Magdalene and Antony van Leeuwenhoek and Tutankhamun and Harriet Tubman would say to each other if they time traveled and ended up discussing the important questions of the day over dinner, snorted contemptuously. Time picked herself up and marched forward, and when she did Abe and Marie flew bass-ackward out the window like balloons suddenly unstrangled. She imagined she knew now why the melted features of the president's face sloped to the side like windblown wax.

Shortly after, History, an opportunist, saw his chance and asked Time out. Time said, "It's over between us," and History said, "But we've never been together," and Time said, "See?"

Some weeks later History thought of a clever comeback, so he phoned Time up and said, in a fleering tone, "One person's past . . . is another's future!" but somehow it didn't sound quite as devastating as it had when he'd practiced it in the mirror, and he quietly replaced the receiver in the cradle and considered giving Space a jingle instead.

History was always trying to fatten time, and Time was always trying to rewrite History. At the moment that this happened, everyone sleeping dreamt they were eating vanilla ice cream made by a ball-bearing manufacturer, and with every lick they chipped their teeth.

After God, Time dated a doctor with a God complex, and they had all the same problems, though he was a little easier to break up with. "Time waits for no man, is that how it is?" he spat at her between belts of bourbon.

A hundred years after Time's sister died, Time thought she saw Emily sitting in a sidewalk café, drinking an iced drink and eating a sandwich in a way that looked very familiar, but the closer she got to her, the more difficult it was to see her, until Time was standing before a table that appeared unoccupied. Time had often thought of asking God if he could bend the rules for her, if she could just once hold Emily's hand again in hers, only for a second, maybe chauffeur her pneuma around on the handlebars of her bicycle, as when they were girls, but she knew he'd never agree to it. What few people knew about God was that he is secretly frightened of revenants, holy or otherwise.

The previous month, two significant things had occurred: an inoculation for the disease that killed Time's sister was developed and a temporal cosmonaut in Russia traveled back in time to visit Peter the Great. Upon the cosmonaut's return to the present, he brought with him a lock of hair that DNA evidence confirmed had indeed been plucked from the head of the czar (while the cosmonaut was there, Peter the Great also practiced his budding dentistry skills on him, and he now had a gaping hole in his smile to prove it). But then strange things began to happen. Ten thousand hirsute men living in St. Petersburg all went suddenly bald on the same day; the blue diadem butterflies of Senegal refused to flap their wings and began to disappear; cabinets of wonder of misshapen men and women and fetal pigs began appearing overnight across Europe and Asia, and long queues of people who felt guilty about their curiosity, but powerless not to slake it, snaked through the cities for miles; and a global potato famine prompted a run on sugar beets and a series of mysterious garrotings on trains traveling to the Urals, which later became known as the Vodka Murders.

Time, who can, when she wants, sprint faster than the naked eye can see, swiped from the research lab a syringeful of the vaccine for her sister's disease, and she found the cosmonaut and ordered him to take her back to her childhood, which he was all too happy to do, he was her biggest fan, he knew her work backward and forward, did she know how long he'd been waiting to meet her? oh, of course, she did! he laughed and reddened. She asked him to take her to a summer night when she and her sister were chasing fireflies in the backyard, and there Time suddenly was, the tire swing twisting on its rope beside her, and there was Emily, holding a blinking net in the air, catching the light she hoped to tame, and Time held Emily's other hand in hers, and it felt cool and smooth like a decorative soap. Emily smiled, then Time quickly jabbed the needle into her sister's eight-year-old arm, but when she did, that simple felicity Time so loved to see slid down Emily's face like rain on a window, and Time's clothes began to unravel and fly apart at the seams, and the earth growled like a large dog and raised its hackles beneath them.

And then God appeared suddenly, very suddenly (which always gave her the jimjams and had been another bone of contention between them), and he sprayed Time with dry ice and froze her in place. He gently moved her hand, careful not to break it off, so the needle withdrew from her sister's arm, and then he exhaled a thawing sirocco, and Time stirred, but she was so startled to see God standing next to her red Radio Flyer wagon she stabbed the needle into his abdomen and pressed the plunger.

Turns out the vaccine for Emily's disease was also an antidote to divinity, and God shrank to the volume and dimensions of a boy and ran through the hedges, and a faint, unidentifiable din shook the air, and bridal bliss calla lilies sprang from the patch of earth on which God had been standing.

God was never seen by Time again.

Time began to wobble, and Emily was no longer beside her, and she thought: *the future is not what it used to be*; it had been altered, and she felt an absence open up in her own history, a revision, a loss, but then she looked at the night sky, as she often did, to bring her out of the spins, and this is what she saw: she saw the winking death that is Emily, that long ago extinction that is burning-bright evidence of a stratospheric future, and she felt less afraid.

When god grew up, he did what he'd wanted to do since before he could remember: he engineered and conducted trains, a beautiful orchestration of brute movement, which is how he'd always imagined God, had there been one. When he came home at night, he kissed his beautiful wife, and for that tender eternity the spheres orbited and sang, all sleeping people dreamt they hung by their feet suspended from a well-meaning hand the size of the moon, and then the world stopped bleeding, and Time felt animal and blameless, a little less fatal, if only for a moment.

Ever After

THE BOOK OF PREDETERMINED NOSTALGIA

It seems like forever and a day, Adam, since we last looked upon one another's transient skins, our final and only parting, your face creased with the exhaustion of a mortality decreed, then forestalled, mine blue with a coming demolition. I was then only seconds away from the blessed inanimation of a new eternity, which I welcomed like the mutineer I was—*murderess*, you said (piqued by a sudden bursitis), *of all future humanity*—sentenced to hard labor in the penal colony of passing time. Were we not to die, to give up those inaugural ghosts, surely we would have wearied of one another in time. Was it really such a terrible thing to have eaten, Knowledge? A girl gets peckish in a garden.

Such ado, it was only a nibble, hardly enough to sustain a sparrow—I came to know a very few things, and one I've never regretted knowing is the body. And shame, which lends a body a decisive circumference. 929 years is, after all, a life long enough to develop regret that it's not shorter, long enough to bury renegade flesh in the hobbling sepulcher of memory. Memory, what we happily lack until it's too late. Imagine, Adam, if we'd had only 70 springs to make good on God's promise. Imagine if the Garden's blooming had had such a clock. Our experience of time might have been delicious. *Life is long*, we said. *Spend as much of it as you can in sleep*, we said. (It is, after all, only sleep that prepares a person not to exist.) *The hay will be there for the making tomorrow*, we said. But the boys didn't listen, insomniac creatures, tapers always burning. Stubborn, like their Grandfather.

The first thousand years are the hardest, said God dryly, when His wrath had dwindled to a nuclear sizzle, the old sobersides. What does He know of a thousand winters of involuntary grief?

929 years, nearly a millennium of atonement, and still He bears a grudge, and so we die and die and die. Forgiveness He leaves to His firstborn (that *other* firstborn, more thirdborn if you ask me), a Johnny-come-lately, whose reanimating martyrdom we can only hope is retroactive. A boy whose bloodless birth will be unsullied by fleshly conception. He'll slip quietly from his mother's immaculate loins like a lima bean from a spoon. Or so I've heard. We thought for a time it might be best never to multiply, remember? Such a vexed mathematics reproduction, thought it best not to bear children only to have them fall from the tree and rot, but one thing a God can ill afford to suffer is fruitlessness (an irony, of course, in my case). Before the coining of humans, God could barely rouse His weary omnipotent amplitude from bed of a morning, but the possibility of being disobeyed fills a moping muleteer with purpose.

This makeshift heaven (something of a celestial inglenook, until God can conjure His marsupial sin swallower, sagging pouch hulking enough to house all iniquity, the beloved Son with his indecisive genes, part stratosphere, part platypus—and who shall bear the sins of the Father? I've always wondered. I confess my liver aches and the bile rises in my throat when I think of it), heaven's steerage, really, is, I must tell you, Adam, not as blue and unbound as you might imagine. There is something resembling the sky that droops above one's head like a tabernacle of blue hair, a mishkan made of the hides of blue goats, and there are walls in the distance but no finitude of course; they are not walls you could ever reach on two human legs or even by the locomotion of divinity (though the gauziest recollection of divining will whisk you away toward a body of water and God's drenching murlimews, so if you wish to remain dry you must forever think desert thoughts. Ack, there I go, sodden again. Being blessed by God is a flounder's game. Also the sunshine is cold as river water in winter, winter itself the fruit of my hunger, and it's easy to catch a chill, though you can never catch your death here. It is part of God's Plan that we feel, like Him, nostalgic for the possibility of perishing. Despite the body's ambivalence at this altitude, there is infirmity here, grippe and ague, chilblains and boils: there is no earthly ailment that compares with the sublime sickness of Paradise).

(It's worth recognizing, though you cannot while yet draped in flesh, that those things that happen parenthetically, those things, dear mortal man, dear husband, are Life. The waiting for life that occurs in the main, that is of course annihilation dissembling.)

Sometimes I miss being disappointed.

THE BOOK OF PARTHENOGENESIS

Remember, Adam, the day I leapt from that beautiful wound that blossomed suddenly in your flank, lovelier than any conciliatory animal God had tossed into Eden (dromedary, pygarg, cankerworm, cockatrice)? God, the old alchemist, always trying out some new alkahest, dripping it on those failed four-bellied inventions of Eden. But me, I was finally gold, transformed (while you were under the anesthesia of God's narcotic breath) from the base metal of manly rib. Adam excerpted. (What They do not tell you is that it was that same rib, the ur-bone, rib of preprimordial Eve, that stirred the mud of you into being, darling, making me bone of your bone of *my* bone, but who's counting? Your provenance is safe with me. *She shall be called Woman, because she was taken out of Man,* etc., but even you, in your willful complacence, can see this is a shell game of the slipperiest sort, since the amputation of *man* from *woman* leaves *wo,* seed of *woe,* seed of *womb,* seed of *wombat, world, worn, wound, wonder,* which self-fertilizes, returning us to the handsome parthenogenesis of *woman,* O! Whereas the subtraction of *man* from *man* leaves, as you can see: O, a dusty void in the lap of bupkis, and that delivers us not from temptation but back where we started, all dressed in tzimtzum with nowhere to go.) And you, so excruciatingly fetching, the chin of a man who knew how to make the sun set, so that he could sleep at the end of an industrious day, hands strong and forever grazing like the husbandry of a bountiful continent, thighs, oh! So ravishing, like the fruitful lands from which our descendants would be banished, tender feet, those of the original nomad blistered with myth and aching with long-fallen arches. Selah!

You had the most poignant lips.

You are Adam, the morning of man, man who comes from all directions, acrostic of God, Arktos Dusis Anatole Mesembria (or North East West South, the first News ever to touch down on Earth), creature conjured of a froth of blood, dust, and gall, elixir of *life*, a word that meant *next to nothing*, you understand, without the possibility of extinction. (One could reason, therefore, it is actually restive Eve who giveth and taketh life.) God, all knowing, knew I'd never be satisfied not knowing, and so it was that He planted me in the Garden, alongside the most innocent stalk of odoriferous rue, knowing knowledge was a tempter He had Himself succumbed to Back in the Day. He was lonely for a fellow criminal, God the loneliest scofflaw this side of Paradise, and me, the original fatal femme, midwife of sin, I hailed from the wrong side of Eden, perfect patsy. I was just the first fatling, Adam. Having the second body on earth, a body built to betray, means you are made for sacrifice and slaughter.

I too grew lonely with the onus of having no predecessor, no scarring childhood, no history to scapegoat, and I fingered your ribs at night, counted those noiseless bones, siblings postponed, and longed to find one missing, a sister seeded somewhere in this stumbling world. *Push*, I whispered furiously into the flesh.

Each time I see God, who always appears to me as the armored tail of an indeterminate animal disappearing beneath a hummock of stones, He tells me a different story about where matter comes from. They sometimes contradict one another, these accounts, and He says they are all true, and then there is the sound of laughter, which I only realize later, my lips reverberant with recollection, fell from my own mouth. He says one morning He woke to find that the burning sun of His belly had begun to contract and whirl, and He stirred the vortex and fingered the molten ylem stewing in His gut, and in the vacuum of light He founded an empty space into which He spat an absence and that absence is us. This made me feel vague, my feet began to vanish, and I had to lie down. I wish you were here, Adam. It is such a chore to exist.

The earth was without form, and void; and darkness was upon the face of the deep. All things were made through Him, and without Him nothing was made that was made. Except sin, made by me, Death's helpmeet.

Another day He tells me something kicked inside Him and He lassoed an empty space nestling in His infinitude and carved it a contour and called it *human*. It made me think of the ostrich that kicked you halfheartedly when you tried to corral it, the world so fallen at that moment we could barely stand.

And then He tells me that time convulsed and the planet was born of a walloping explosion, the beginning of anything a matter of strategic violence, and we began as tadpoles, who one day left the sanctuary of water, developed sturdy legs and shed our gills, and braved the land, and over time we stood upright and began to scheme.

THE BOOK OF ZOOLOGOS

Oh, and remember the naming of the animals? God brought to you the beasts of the field and the fowl of the air and said call them what you will, and so you took me around on that first day and schooled me in your zoology. Stroking their muzzles and tapping their bills, you said, *carburetor, Millard Fillmore, ham on rye, Armageddon, ode to joy, pinochle, bone spurs, fumaroles, milk teeth, catastrophe,* and I offered this revision: *cormorant, mountain goat, horse leech, golden calf, ossifrage, palmer worm, basilisk, fallow deer, turtle dove, chameleon, moo moo moo!* God had a fondness for your lexicon, though, and kept a would-be meme or two for Himself.

Such power we had then to affect the future of history, the outcome of all things, when the very atmosphere was young and impetuous. How little we knew, but that was precisely the rub, wasn't it? Had we known, perhaps we might not have longed to know. I know, I should speak for myself. You were content to be the Garden's starveling, innocence your meat and drink.

If God does not regret inventing a creature He knew would doom humanity, how can I regret being that creature, mere villainess in a drama foretold, necessary anarchist? I am only the radicle of mortality. Mortification does not come naturally to a girl set down among the lilies, in a garden smelling, seductively, of bdellium (adulterant of myrrh), botany of love. If God did not make me do it, does that mean my will superseded His? How I long to be remorseful! Would that theology did not forbid it.

On the subject of the so-called serpent: *Serpent* is what you first called that cunning budmash and later, before our expulsion, I suggested *turtle*, a word that sounds like rain when you sing it. It was a snapping turtle that turned my head, that slow-moving provocateur. A turtle is a good deal more subtle than what we eventually christened *serpent*, a sibilant name whose hiss you became attached to, a name that has hitched its wagon to our infamy, while turtles of every stripe have burrowed in the mud and escaped scrutiny entirely.

So the turtle clacked his beak and said to me,

—Do you not long to be God?

And I said I hadn't given it much thought, having existed only a short while and never having had a father who dandled me on his knee.

—I haven't any ambitions, I said.

The turtle scratched the ground and sniffed.

—History will never speak of the burden of being a paragon.

—I suppose not, I said.

—History? I said.

Then he urged me only to pluck from that tree the unauthorized fruit that glistened like early evening, and split it open.

—Only that, he said.

I did as he asked and heard no thunderclap and felt slighted.

He said, —The burden of history will never be as onerous as the burden of no history. Unlike you and Adam, he said, retracting his bald bobbling noggin, taking cover, God is *all* childhood.

I said, —I know.

I said, —History?

He said to shake the halves, and when I did the seeds leapt to the ground.

—You cannot sow seeds in a garden that never withers, he said.

He said, —A thoughtful death is a grander destiny than a life lived in unripening ignorance.

And you know, Adam, how susceptible I always was when the subject of fate arose.

When the turtle's reptilian eye slowly blinked, it looked like a waxing moon, and I ate the fruit, which was sweeter than the comeliest cherry, sweeter than the green blood of the heart that never stops beating, sweeter by far than immortality.

We did not cover ourselves. That is the invention of a timid amanuensis, who found his own shriveled fig so homely he feared even the most robust woman who gazed upon it would die instantly of fright.

There would be so many other things to be ashamed of.

THE BOOK OF POSTPRANDIAL EXPULSION

And God's voice walked on two hairy legs through the garden, whistling, and when you saw it, you blurted, —We did not eat the forbidden fruit! Whereupon God's two-legged voice scuffled to and fro, kicking so much debris into the air that the sun was dimmed, and I was struck deaf as driftwood. Your legs shook, and you pointed at me.

Suddenly all the flowers and trees and animals flew into the air and churned above us, tornado of a nullified bliss, and I heard the fevered lowing of cows, who are made so easily dizzy. *You shall eat dirt!* bellowed God. *You shall gorge on unending sorrow!* And God's notorious temper at that moment set the young sky ablaze and caused all living creatures, save you and me, to granulate particle by particle and return to the flinders of pre-being.

And with one well-wound sidewinder from the voice of God, out of Paradise we bounced.

THE BOOK OF DISABLED LAMENTATIONS

The garden knocked out of me, I began to bleed, and you feared I'd lose all color and turn to water, and you swabbed me in a poultice of turmeric and carotene. Years later we would come to know that I'd miscarried, the tissue of unfallen humanity spilling from me in clots. My belly ached, but it was not a terrible feeling. Every month I asked the blood to revisit me, and it did. But then one day it stopped, and during those months when I could not summon it, I ate sugar beets and drank molasses and waited for emptiness to return. My belly bowed like the throat of a bullfrog at midnight.

When the boys appeared, I tried not to hold it against them that they'd taken my blood and thickened it, turned it to flesh. The beauty of blood is that it sleeps through the night and never asks to be fed.

Because we'd had no childhoods ourselves, we did not know what it was we were to do with these puzzling manikins that seemed more mollusk than human, too short and clumsy to be of any help during a harvest, and we stored them like potatoes in a dark place.

It was Abel who was inconsolable as a boy. His cheeks flushed and damp, he reminded me of a bowl of radishes, toward which I've always felt sentimental. *We are all alone in the universe, we are all alone,* he lamented day after day after interminable day. He held the fatted fowl in his lap and cried before he broke their necks. He was the only one of us who understood what it meant to be irremediably mortal. Doomed fowl are not indifferent to their plight (on its last day the pheasant waves its wattle in surrender). They know when their lives have come to an end and curl like the fists of infants just before they are slaughtered.

Cain was a happy child, the spitting image of you as a boy, had you ever been a boy, which was more than God could bear. He would never again look at your aboriginal face, nor forgive you for listening to the legless voice of a woman. I, being the very shape and girth of innocence, listened to a crafty reptile I had no reason to distrust (God had said nothing instructive about turtles), but *you* listened to the lesser sex, a shadow of doubt forever after darkening the supremacy of he who harbors no eggs. That was the test we failed. Since then the mere mention of woman makes God dyspeptic.

God is a man's thing. How to survive God's love, a woman's.

I have seen our Abel here walking dreamily in the distance, always amidst the sheep, of which there is a strange bounty in this floating interim. Cain I have seen neither hide nor hair of, and this troubles me. How many times did we warn that headstrong whelp that God was a being nourished on blood sausage and sweetbreads? With no health to fret the loss of, He happily consumed the fat of the fattest fatted calf, we told him, and still Cain stubbornly insisted a well-tended parsnip would woo God just as readily as a shank of mutton. But God does not bother with bloodless victuals. He has, after all, a fallen world to fuel, and the guilty are infinitely famished.

When we were yet childless, I dug up a pale tuber that was plump like a little man, and I kept it in my pocket, where I supposed all children spent their early lives so that they would not broil in the sun or be washed away in a deluge and could expand into proper Eves and proper Adams, but then it went soft, and I feared the same would happen to Cain when he finally appeared (I know I bellowed at a pitch that caused the color to drain from your cheeks, so that your face looked like dusk approaching, but the pain of childbirth is, as promised, wonderfully agonizing, a reminder of the anesthetic bliss a fatally curious girl forfeits when she steps foot outside the safe haven of Paradise, the Garden that place where torment is never allowed to mature, and when Cain clawed his way free of me, I thought of all the snakes I'd watched skinning themselves new). So I buried him in the ground up to his startled mouth, out of which an intermittent storm flew, and when he grew quiet as a yam, you dug him up, Adam, and laid him in my arms, a hungry bundle of kindling.

Abel mourned every death, even that of the fallen leaves, the trampled clover, the mayflies he saw drop from the air after a day of life, the sky that bled to death each night. It was all Abel thought about, perishing, and then he began to long for his own end, so tired was he of anticipating it, son of my sin, but he did not long to displease God and could never bring his hand to his own throat. And on that day when God informed Cain that his offering and faith were paltry, Abel came to Cain and boasted that his tender veal had left God well pleased. It was unlike Abel to spit poison in the face of his brother (who had indeed been his keeper when they were children, Abel so willfully feeble and prone to earache, Cain stout as a tree stump), and Cain knew this, but he'd inherited a certain hotheaded bluster and worked himself into a ferment easy as breathing, and so he drew his knife of chalcedony, recently sharpened, and just then I happened upon them and watched as Abel launched himself at Cain and ran himself through, the knife receiving a glad reception from those organs that yearned to be perforated. Abel died in Cain's arms, and his face shone with gratitude. When God investigated Abel's disappearance, Cain fled His scrutiny as long as he could but eventually confessed to having committed the world's first homicide (or was it to spare his brother's memory from the ignominy of the high treason of self-extinction? Abel the first to preempt God in that way), and God roared with an incinerating fury, scorching that season's crops to cinder. And thus evil was born on the earth.

THE BOOK OF GENETIC REVELATION

I gave up children for a time, and when Seth stanched the blood in my belly, I was already a centenarian. I pretended he was a girl, eyes like garnets, and we stayed in the zenana, just two girls in exile (one in the diaspora of exile), and hummed like the nearby freshet, the sound it sang when thawing. Eventually I ransomed my happiness to his boyhood, but he continued to smile bashfully and stare at his delicate feet, even after hair sprouted on his chest and made him itch.

Our children paired off and bore their own squalling potatoes, and that was the beginning of the world. We were uncle son sister cousin mother to one another, though I would never be anyone's daughter. When you are related to every upright creature on earth, there is precious little opportunity to escape your own blood, which trails you like a lost cur, tail down, nose to the ground.

One day the world will be a great garboil of iniquity and God will feel penitent unto Himself for having seeded it (*Forgive me, Father*, He will whisper to Himself on calloused knee; *You are pardoned, my Son*, He will respond, but He will consider asphyxiating Himself with his own omniscience, which does on occasion provoke pulmonary complaint. When the child is father of the man, there are, if you ask me, two people too many in the room, and a twinned psyche that capacious naturally unspools when forced to stare itself in the limitless mug), for having germinated this bipedal race born of the sons of God and the daughters of men, born in blood after pecking free of the shell of woman's soft-boiled belly. Men will see stones shaped like the end of the world, and they will stop to worship them prophylactically, and giants will roam the earth and eat the hearts of trees, pollard their tender crowns to leafless splinters and leave the rest, and trees everywhere will begin to wither and the air in the world will grow thin and unnourishing. And all our children and children's children, born with the birth defect of being human, born to fallen guardians, will live in violence, sensing there once had been a life of unending splendor and ease and amity, where the notion of suffering pricked no living creature's imagination (except, of course, that of the turtle), and then earthly brutality will couple with the ferocity of a disappointed sovereign and beget the diluvian purge—*And GOD saw that the wickedness of man was great in the earth, and that every imagination of the thoughts of his heart was only evil continually*—and He will vomit water everywhere upon the land, so that when the earth gasps, water will fill its lungs and drown it in the rising sea. But. A tiny vessel of salvaged life will weather His wet wrath. (As will, of course, the turtle, crack swimmer, master of rapids.)

THE BOOK OF MENDED OBLIVION

I tell you this, Adam, because you are in your final year and will soon join me, and once you arrive here among the first and newly dead, awaiting a retroactive salvation, you are powerless to right any earthly wrong, but there is yet time to antidote our expulsion, if only you can find the Tree of Ignorance. I've heard tell it is a gnarled and sickly thing, its fruit most bitter, but you must eat of it only once and our race will be struck witless once again, knowledge trickling out of our ears, falling from our wrists, and evaporating in the insensible ether of a rehabilitated Paradise! The trees all around you will spring so quickly into bloom they will appear at first to be blighted with growth, hideously lush, that pestilent abundance we can scarcely recall; the tarnished sky will silver then grow unthinkably blue once again; and my life, our lives, will be reversed, that rotten apple returned to its glistening limb, original sin unspun, whereupon I will climb back into the garden's uncorrupted womb, hermetic and snug, and wait, Adam, to be summoned from your bones for the making of a benighted breed, wait for a refurbished eternity to ripen on the vine, and wait, dear Adam dear Adam dear Adam, and wait, dear Adam, and wait.

KANSAS

The Middle

Is forever west of where you are.

Telling the Chicken

The skinny is this: last night I dreamt of chickens, glowing fat and white. They were spinning in circles on the tips of their tangerine claws, their feet and legs a thorny axis. They whirled, beaks skyward, and feathers flew. They were perfect in their gyrations, as if their movements had been divined by some force long ago, when cosmic laws were set. And I thought to myself, this is what happens when the magnetic fields reverse, an event for which I have been waiting patiently for quite some time.

It gets hotter than Dutch love in Lucas, Kansas, in August. The cicadas scream with the heat. Public records tell us it was 112°F here on August 18, 1909, so the planet's warming hasn't touched us much, though the rest of the world seems to be catching up. I've got my eye on those polar ice caps.

Lotta was a bona fide beauty. She had bobbed, black hair and skin white as the blood of a milkweed, so clear and clean it made you want to go home and take a bath. When Lotta got sick, her lips went funny. They were thick and lovely, bee-stung, but a wet brown-blood color would rush into them at night, and they looked like pieces of raw liver. Sometimes my heart ached so bad for Lotta, I wanted to take her head into my mouth and hide her from herself.

The Garden of Eden is located here in Lucas. In the summer, curious tourists flock to gander at the concrete rendering of the famed creation. I must admit it is impressive. The brittle, reposed body of the Garden's architect and sculptor is preserved in a glass case in the backyard. Age-wise he appears to have given Methuselah a run for his money. Lotta and I would often sit beneath a long stretch of concrete serpent and discuss the wages of sin. Her papa was an occasional minister at the Open Door Baptist Church.

Lucas is only a nod and holler from Cawker City, where the Largest Ball of Twine sits proud and bulbous. It's something you can be part of, this ball of twine, you can be responsible for making it larger, securing its spot in the *Guinness Book of Records,* so no made-in-a-day coastal ball can squeeze it out of its rightful place. When Lotta died, I drove to Cawker City and donated a fair bit of fine hemp in her name. They wound it on right then and there with a makeshift rod and spool device. The ball of twine is big and round as anything. Its bulging symmetry makes your eyes water.

Lotta's papa was a chicken farmer. He could balance an egg on its end even when it wasn't the vernal equinox. When Lotta died, he gave me a gross of fertile eggs. Sometimes I crack them open in private and touch the blood spots.

Lotta's papa killed all the chickens except one. He cracked neck after neck, loaded them into trash bags, drove them to the church parking lot, and flung the caboodle of them into the mouth of the dumpster. The one he kept was Lotta's favorite, a fancy bantam. It rode her shoulder and whispered sweet things in her ear, nibbling at the kernel of her lobe. When Lotta fell sick, it took to walking in circles like a carnival pony. Lotta's papa coddled it after the funeral. He blew on its beak and massaged its feet. He asked me if I'd talk to it, try to explain what had happened.

I took the chicken to the Garden. It wouldn't stay on my shoulder, so I held it under my arm. It knew the blond hair it tugged at was not Lotta's. I pointed to the long, skinny figure of Eve. "People blame a heap of heartache on her," I said, "but I don't think she had any foresight of histoplasmosis." The chicken kicked, then went limp, crossing over from denial to acceptance.

Everyone's lawns are jaundiced with heat. Sometimes with the last hot gasp of summer we get quick, hard rains and comet-sized hail, but not this time. The street is no place to fry an egg, despite the TV meteorologist's suggestion.

I am taking shepherd's pie to Lotta's papa tonight. He has bought the chicken a toy piano. He will prod it to play with a handful of mash on the keys. It will peck out an unfamiliar tune, then turn round and round till the next request. Lotta's papa will sing about the sweet sound of grace, the chicken will roll on its back with a soft gurgle of clucks, and we'll both rub its stomach.

Tonight the world will turn on its ear, chicken, I can feel it. Glaciers will thaw and drip, fat magnets will fly up toward a shower of stars, and a shiver of moist dreams will shake me awake as eggs crack and scatter.

Kansas

What Kansas most hated about herself was that she was irrepressibly wholesome and incapable of sleeping in on Sundays. She also fretted that that record-breaking ball of twine on display in Cawker City marked her like an unsightly goiter. Seemed the older she got, the more roadside attractions she accumulated. So it was with aging. She thought about this as she tried to lean unprimly against the wall and nibbled on a carrot stick at the annual all-state cocktail party. New Jersey, that scurrilous wag, had made a joke whose lasciviousness she detected too late, something about boning, and she'd impulsively quipped that she was a femur's daughter. (It was thought by some, those sniffy wiseacres that believed a book's cover told them everything they needed to know, that she lacked a sense of humor, a belief it had been hard to shake since those dry days when she'd protested the imbibing of spirits. She now admitted on this point she may have been a stubborn holdout—"A trifle doctrinaire!" Illinois once huffed—though she stood by her belief in Election Day and Sabbath sobriety. Now, in her dotage, she herself indulged in a pony glass of cordial from time to time, held it demonstratively in the air at hootenannies such as this one, which met with eye rolling and made her feel like the most scorned and fraudulent kind of tenderfoot. How was it a state so central could be made to feel so marginal?) She'd immediately regretted having spoken to New Jersey at all, which was often the case, and then she saw the look on his soon-to-erupt face, a potluck look of having taken a mouthful of something unidentifiable he couldn't wait to spit in his napkin when unobserved, and she glowed red as the tasseled corn on which an August dusk has alit. *Quelle naïf*, scoffed Louisiana, who'd been snide and territorial ever since the Purchase. Well, didn't Kansas just feel like a bolt of gingham, mercy.

She watched New York sashay like the cock of the walk, as he was in a habit of doing, his fetching silver hair shimmering like a thousand moonlit lakes. Once, some years ago, he'd invited her for a visit: "Hey Kansas, come to the big city, get out and live a little, doll, see what you're missing. We're the fly-to, not the flyover," he'd said, elbowing her in what she feared would seem to him like corn-fed ribs, and he'd promised to take her to a Broadway revival of *Oklahoma*, which had always been a favorite of hers, so she threw caution to the wind and said, oh, what the heck! "The time is nigh!" he'd quipped. NY, har. He could be a charmer, that one, slick as snake oil. She ended up in an unscrupulous cab (she was up to date in her thinking and therefore did not believe the corruption of the cabbie could be blamed on the Romani people) and had had to fork over all the pin money she had hidden beneath a sock in her pocket. She'd been taught that trick by Nebraska, who seemed somehow to know her way around the mean streets of the world. Kansas always consulted Nebraska before traveling anywhere.

She'd found New York, dashing rogue, an interesting state to visit, but, mmmm, well, she wouldn't want to live there and was happy to return to the snoozy flatness of home, unruffled as it was by the swagger and glitz of freshly rehabbed celebrities and sullen artists who construct pietàs out of flank steak and doll parts. Honestly, these citified onions need a hobby, thought Kansas. Nothing wrong with them that a good sewing circle and a tuna noodle casserole couldn't cure. (Though Kansas could boast her own share of the famous and clever, had she a mind to brag, her humble cities did not feel the need to chisel in the sidewalk the name of every Tom, Dick, and Agnes Moorehead who'd spent a debauched night inside the state lines, like that be-arched and self-doubting child of Missouri's, who has never recovered from the heady inebriation of the World's Fair, its brief and shining moment a century ago, pity.)

Oh, horsefeathers, there was that cur Missouri now, with whom she had a long and difficult history, who had once caused Kansas to bleed (though he refused to rehash those hemorrhagic days of yore with her now, *blood under the bridge*, he'd say with a growl), a history and proximity from which no restraining order could save her. He twirled his waxed moustache and leered at her, knowing she had no choice but to tolerate his impertinence, given their shared custody of little latchkey Kansas City. He tossed her a narrow-eyed nod, and she backpedaled so hastily she bumped into Texas, oof, whose sizable caboose was always stalled on someone's tracks. Texas's plate was, as usual, piled high with victuals, appetite and ego both big as, well, Texas. That's one state that could do with a little calorie counting, thought Kansas, lay off the longhorn T-bone and toast, opt instead for some lean chicken and a spear of broccoli or two, maybe a smidgen of blackberry slump from time to time, to get some fruit in his diet, do that tub's arteries a world of good. Well, she could hardly talk. It had been a long time since she was a mere slip of a territory, some years since she could shimmy her backside into the slender frontier duds of her youth. No, she'd gained a few since then. Those hardy farmhands and prairie preachers liked their pot roast and potatoes and apple pan dowdy come Sunday, and she had the waistline to prove it. She could never again wear horizontal stripes nor anything that accentuated those childbearing hips of hers.

California, now there was a state that could eat absolutely anything and never gain an ounce, which Arizona believed would not continue to be the case unless the immigration laws were stiffened. "Hey, Kansas, got your green*horn* card on ya?" gibed Arizona once, a real comedian that one. Kansas didn't think the nation should let just any yahoo cross our borders, but she, being of welcoming attitude toward all industrious pioneers, had given sanctuary to many a displaced inhabitant, of various heritages, herself and found them to be fine, hardworking folk, and she didn't believe the country's many ills could be laid at the feet of the undocumenteds, though you wouldn't catch her spouting such socialistical notions publicly, no siree bobhope. Speaking of unpopular ideas, she sure missed that old fire-eyed sword swallower John Brown, though naturally she dared not even think such a thing in the presence of Virginia. He'd had the most handsome neck, a principled neck, straight and stalwart as a silo, snapped like a steeple in a storm in the end. Never had she regretted the invention of the gallows so keenly. Well, his methods left something to be desired, no doubt about it, but those had not been days of fruitful diplomacy, and she'd watched him grow ever-more lean with violent resolve when it seemed blood was the only language in which the country was fluent. Oh, dear, she always got nostalgic in large gatherings. Dear John Brown now lies a molder-ing in the soil of New York, chided old New York, who never missed an opportunity to remind her of this fact when the states started waxing fondly about their youths. Things just hadn't gone as she'd hoped, and she had in fact risked a little hope back in the day when the Exodusters, fleeing the threat of a second bondage, had made their way to the promising refuge of her, had *flocked* to Kansas, veritable droves of refugees thought Kansas was the place to be, and then she'd briefly nursed hope again when the plains were radically aflame with those wild-eyed agrarian crusaders. Nope, things had taken an unfortunate turn. A believer in the fate of a name, Kansas thought it was no coincidence that, a century later, it was little Linda Brown who would take on those muttonheaded Topekans determined to force the state to stick to its hateful yokel-hood. Something else she didn't like to admit was how little affection she harbored for her capitol. She wasn't sure where she'd gone wrong with that rabid pulpiteer, holy moly.

Yes, blood under the bridge, she supposed. These days she knew well the role she played as an inveterate red state, and it was too late in the game to blue it up now and tip the scales. Those arrogant coasts— made smug by a little waterfront property, piffle, those on the side where the sun rose claiming to have their righteous colonial finger on the pulse since day one—they had to be held in check somehow. Hello? Ever hear of the witch trials? Now *that* had been a proud and progressive historical moment, had it not? Those Mayflower wisenheimers. Actually, Kansas had a soft spot for the Puritans, but she'd burned nary a witch in her day she felt compelled to point out for the record when accused of intolerance, which really got her goat. Has anyone taken a census in Lawrence lately? Tol-erance didn't begin to cover it. That was a city that welcomed all manner of peculiarity, as college towns tended, on misguided principle, to do. Was it really necessary to be a card-carrying oddball to teach college? Tolerance schmolerance, fruitcake is fruitcake, and who wanted to sit next to that at the Ponderosa? Change your shirt, comb your mop, quit muttering into your beard, and make some sense for Pete's sake. While she was glad that that unpleasant House Un-American Activities business was behind us, she knew which of her cities would make the list should another Tail Gunner Joe ever rise to power and start to sniff out unsavory sympathies. Give her a school with an agronomy major any dadgum day of the week. Massachusetts had once accused her of being an ag hag, and she'd sputtered, *I know you are, but what am I?* Not one of her finer rhetorical moments, to be sure, but where does that Maotsechusetts (she'd gotten that one from that old porch swing punster Mississippi) get off insinuating she'd been left behind in the postindustrial dust? Anyway, Lawrence, Lawrence, you can give your children all the guidance in the world, but they choose their own path in the end, and it might just lead to Vermont, heaven forfend, but what are you going to do? It's a free country. How many times had she heard that at a board meeting? *Don't I know it. Maybe we ought to start charging*, she'd jested, yukkity-yuk: dead silence. These were the cutups who said *she* wanted for a sense of humor. Oh, she had a sense of humor. You don't live through countless supercell tornadoes further flattening your fruited plains, and host all those UFO and Airstream trailer conventions, without having a sense of humor, oh, no, you certainly do not.

Good gravy Marie, these reunions took it out of her. She was one wheel down and an axle dragging. Social situations caused her insecurities to itch around the throat like a woolen turtleneck (which she hated; she much preferred a v-neck in a synthetic blend, however unnatural). She was a homebody at heart, always had been. Thank goodness she knew enough to keep her trap shut in mixed company. *Watermelonwatermelonwatermelonlalala*, she chanted to herself as she made her way across the room, to keep from being drawn into social intercourse. At the last Christmas-Hanukah-Kwanzaa-all-purpose-heathen celebration, she'd gotten a little tipsy on the green sherbet punch that South Dakota brought and that the District of Columbia, who'd crashed the gala demanding to be recognized and who everyone knew was a serious tippler, had spiked, that ornery cuss, and she'd stood on the table and started to sing, belligerently, *O Little Town of Bethlehem*. She was all for inclusivity, but did that really mean those lovely crèches with their plaster-of-paris baby Jesuses and wise men and doe-eyed Marys would now and forever have to gather dust in the basements of all state buildings, go begging for all eternity? She understood why people got het up about the Confederate flag waving its freighted *X* in front of a capitol dome, but what, pray tell, had little Jesus ever done to anybody? Was it his fault some cockamamie ignoramuses twisted his words to suit their poison? She didn't think so. Shoot the message, but don't hate the messenger, people! She was feeling discombobulated now. These affairs always scrambled her thinking like eggs in a morning mess hall.

Oh, nuts, Colorado was headed her way and was sure to drag her blasted purple mountains majesty into the conversation, as she did at every opportunity—little Rockies this, showing off their altitude, and, land sakes, you should have seen the Rockies that, blah-biddyblah—and to insinuate that Kansas was somehow responsible for the flatness of her eastern border, a regular assassin of picturesque landscapes. Seemed somebody was always pointing a finger, the nerve. Sometimes Kansas thought of Colorado as an obstinate wrinkle someone ought to just take a hot iron to once and for all. *Talk about making a mountain out of a molehill*, she'd said to Colorado once. She *had* a sense of humor. No doubt *Co-co*, as she liked to be called (which caused collective eyes to roll, not just hers, and in fact Kansas never took Colorado directly to task for putting on airs, was always polite as pie to her face; that was the code of the Midwest and she abided by it), was going to try to lobby votes in the evolution debate, egged on by Tennessee, of course, who'd all but outlawed the word *monkey* in public discourse. Really Kansas, though she knew the position some of her less science-minded denizens insisted on, couldn't understand what all the hoo-ha was about when it came to evolution and creationism. If we'd all once been eyeless salamanders staggering out of the briny deep, couldn't we just agree that God had seen fit for us to start thusly? Maybe there'd be no Johnny Weissmuller, no Esther Williams, had we started differently. Maybe gifted swimmers had genetic memory buried in their limbs. And weren't rugged, winsome, plum-lipped actors (Louise Brooks, that comely Pandora, born and bred in Cherryvale, KS) gifted in synchronized movements a boon to the human race? Had anyone ever thought of that (she did love the old movies, those days of uncomplicated ermined glamour, had a collection of old *Photoplays* at home)? She could see an advantage or two to having once had gills. Maybe the Garden of Eden had just, you know, grown its fallen perfection on another side of the planet, and those two lines eventually met up, fell in love, and gave birth to humanity as we know it today. Or something like that, she hadn't worked out the details yet. Course she didn't want anyone thinking she was endorsing any kind of intermixing of the bestial and bipedal classes, no, she'd have to think that one through a little more. In any case, there was always a compromise position to be had (as that dastard Missouri well knew). A stubborn inflexibility of principles so often resulted in the most dunderheaded legislation: requiring a hunting license to capture mice, say, or making it illegal for a woman to doff clothing beneath the portrait of a man, the stately stare of a jowly patriarch no doubt inciting the most lascivious thoughts in the woman as she shimmies free of her petticoat, arf (Ohio'd been given no small amount of grief about that one over the years. *Get a load of this!* Nevada would say as she walked by all those gilt-framed presidential portraits and flashed fishnetted thighs in Ohio's direction. Kansas thought Nevada was really a closet introvert, possibly even dowdy in her off-hours, despite those false eyelashes she batted, like a duck coming in for a landing and all those compulsive behaviors, because she often ended up sobbing into her gimlet by the end of the evening. Definitely looking for love in all the wrong places, that one). Oh, Colorado just got buttonholed by Wyoming, probably playing landscape one-upsmanship, praise cheese and crackers!

Gadzooks, Kansas had a doozy of a headache. There were tiny ice picks of light stabbing at her eyes, and she could feel her sinuses pulsing. She seemed to spend half the year nasally compromised. Smack dab in the middle of the allergy belt, she found hay fever season had her honking her horn for months on end, all that deceptively cheerful goldenrod spreading unchecked across the plains. She was going to try inconspicuously to duck into the cloakroom, fetch her wrap, and slip into the night unnoticed, God willing and the creek don't rise.

She parted the coats and, oh, there was Idaho! Sitting in the closet by himself, looking as unpopulous as Montana, dreaming, she knew, of Wyoming, who had blackened Idaho's come-hither eye at last year's party. Kansas tried to smile at him and wished she could tell him that she personally didn't give two hoots about what two consenting states did in the privacy of their own borders, but she knew it would likely sound false coming from her, what with some of her most vocal citizens barking so hatefully on the subject. If there were anything that wearied her more than those constituents' grim devotion to the End Times, she couldn't think of what it would be. Lordamercy, how they loved a brimstone scenario, those merry apocalyptics, looked upon world unrest as evidence that the prescience of Revelation and Nostradamus and the Mayans was upon us, and bring it on! When their predictions mandated they build Styrofoam pyramids and keep a nightly vigil to scan the skies for the silver spaceships that would ferry them to the Afterlife, she found herself nostalgic for the simpler times of backyard bomb shelters stocked with a lifetime supply of tallow candles, Twinkies, and condensed milk, the Red Menace lying in ambush under every mattress, waiting to spring on democracy as soon as it slept. That threat at least had an address you could send a postcard to, *Freedom is here, wish you were beautiful.* Now it seemed like folks feared everything, however tabloid, just to be on the safe side. Oh, these upstart modern times, they did make a body bone tired. She was beat as a rented mule. Kansas quickly found her stole and gave Idaho a sympathetic, if noncommittal, nod on her way out.

She was two feet from freedom when she felt a tap on her shoulder. It was Colorado, rat finks! who told her she was wanted in the Continental Room. Kansas hemmed and hawed a bit, tried to scratch up a plausible excuse for being the first to flee, then Colorado said, okay, if she had to know, she was going to receive an award. "An award?" asked Kansas, blink-blinking in the dim light of the foyer. One reason she'd wanted to quietly secede from this reunion was because she always received exactly bupkis at the awards ceremony at the end of the night. All the usual suspects walked away with the golden statuettes every year, while her mantel continued to collect only dust. She felt herself flush red as the head of Rita Hayworth at the thought, and she began to giggle and stumble about like a moony schoolgirl on roller skates. "Me," she asked, "are you sure?" One year she'd received the award for most promising silver-tongued governor, but it was instantly clear to everyone that this had been a typo, and with a leaden heart she surrendered it to Arkansas, who tried hard not to gloat until Kansas was pushed to the back by the circle of glad-handing congratulators.

Co-co grabbed her by the arm, ushered her back, and whispered, "Gonna be your night, no more playing Kick the Kansas," and Kansas choked back a sob. Could it be her sideline diplomacy and (albeit reserved) congeniality (who was it brought snickerdoodles and s'mores to *every* tiresome fireside chat) had finally been recognized for the low-profile but essential consensus-building assets they were? Would the trusty tortoise finally win the race? Any time Kansas edged close to any kind of long-overdue recognition, she thought of her airborne prodigy Amelia Earhart soaring in the skies over exotic, grass-skirted locales not often frequented by Kansas girls, thought of her disappearing into the side of a sunlit mountain, and it choked her right up. Amelia, Amelia! thought Kansas.

Colorado sat Kansas down at her table, and she saw that Iowa, for some reason, would not look at her. Probably just a twinge of jealousy, as Iowa, thought to be plain and simple as a burlap bag, was similarly misunderstood. Nevada grinned her radioactive grin from the next table and twirled in her fingers a paper umbrella. Everyone's eyes were boozily a-droop, and the ceremony was winding down. New York, emceeing as he did every year, was falling back on some Borscht Belt shtick (he'd taken her to the Catskills when she'd visited, which she'd enjoyed, except for all those wife-hating jokes. She didn't think that line of needling was necessary, had felt somehow personally implicated by those wisecracks New York tried hard not to hoot at), and then he said, "And now for the long-awaited final award of the evening," and Kansas pricked up her ears. "The prize for best sense of humor"—oh, this was a new category of recognition entirely! And as it was the final prize of the evening . . . Kansas looked at her dear neighbor Colorado, who she could see was trying not to beam prematurely, and there was Missouri, sitting at a table near the front, stroking his chin and glaring at her through the slits of his envious eyes, and in fact all eyes were on her! –"the prize for best sense of humor goes"—New York opened the envelope ceremoniously and said, "Oh, the dark horse places at last! This year's prize goes to my good friend from the Middle Kingdom: Kansas!"

Saints preserve us! Kansas found herself rising wobbly to her feet, and then everyone stood with her, and her ears filled with the sound of their booming, their adoring applause. Dear Amelia! said Kansas to herself, the sound catching in her throat, and she thought too in this moment, one of the finest in her statehood, that John Brown (though not especially known for his madcap antics) was also there beside her, witness to justice. She felt his righteous spirit in the quickened beat of her heart. And then she saw the shoulders of everyone around her begin to shudder like jackhammers, moved to tears they were! and New York regained his composure and said, *Oh, I'm sorry, oops, I seem to have read the wrong line, my bad! The award actually goes to . . . Colorado! Whose idea it was to award Kansas the prize for best sense of humor! Hawhawhaw . . .*

Kansas saw the faces around her collapse in hilarity as the states bent at the waists and beat their knees, Colorado, Missouri, Massachusetts, California, even Nebraska, that turncoat! They brayed like donkeys and wiped the streaming tears from their cheeks, and in that moment Kansas, a long-time defender of the right to bear arms, took out the automatic weapon of her imagination and gunned down every last smug and bullying, sanctimonious, superior star on the American flag, spraying bullets as though she were just sowing seed, becoming again the wild gunslinger she had been in those law-less days of her girlhood. In her mind she plugged each and every one of them full of lead and watched them drop to the ground like wet sacks of sorghum, but outwardly she remained stoic as a silo in December. She would not give these scurrilous scoundrels the sat-isfaction of seeing her wear her broken heartland on her sleeve.

Colorado, New York, Nevada clapped her on the back, and one by one the states circled around her and told her what a good sport she was, shook her hand, socked her jovially on the arm, and, what was this, she saw—could it be?—admiration in their eyes, deference even? Why yes! She was certain she espied approval in the way they coughed into their shoulders and sighed and smiled, approval of the good-natured, trouperish way she had handled this ribbing, admi-ration for how she always soldiered on in the face of disappoint-ment, and it was true, that was part of having a very good sense of humor, wasn't it, being able to be the butt of the jocularity of others (however cheap) with aplomb, to take being made sport of in stride? This made Kansas's heart leap modestly in her chest and she decided to hang up the hardware and take those turn-the-bruised-cheek teachings to heart.

She felt herself fairly vibrating with forgiveness as she walked toward the door inside a cozy circle of radiance, whose heat she could feel on her scalp, and she lapped up the grace of finally having made it to that inner circle of love and high regard, as though she were one of the original colonies, the Dirty Thirteen as they were affectionately known, to that golden place where your chin was chucked and your hair tousled and you were accepted for the some-times gullible but quick-witted, good-humored, *necessary* bumpkin you were. And as she felt herself rise into the pinkening clouds of a perfect new dawn, into the welcoming embrace of posterity, she lowered her goggles, set her throttle toward eternity, and waved at the disappearing patchwork below her.

The Rising Girl

after Dino Buzzati

Matilda was tall. Feet big and attentive as wolfhounds, flattening the groomed grass in front of the skyscraper, she peered into a third-story window, then looked at the sky shining shamelessly above her, so cloudless it made her totter. The sun was somewhere in full bloom, incendiary petals wavering, and she sometimes thought it would be a reassuring darkness, to lose her eyes to an indelible light, but she stared instead at her feet, which as far as she knew had never blinded anyone.

Matilda threw her gaze across the improbable state of Kansas, as though she were scattering morning mash among the chickens, and what she saw were autumn fields, long fallow, awaiting a cor-roborating frost; a vandalized church, bits of colored glass winking beneath the windows like candy, where the sound of the spirit had once hummed with enough vigor to interfere with the nighttime navigation of planes; winter-rusted trucks, cars dragging exhaust pipes like sullen animals with broken tails, and aimless combines throwing dirt behind them on dusty roads; enervated rabbits lying tail to tail with few predators to flee from; the occasional cow, empty mouth vigilantly grinding its ghost cud, planted on the spot where she last saw her calf; a police car flashing behind a dying deer or or-phaned opossums clinging to a rotting log in the middle of the road; and this skyscraper, tall as the moon and bulging with indoor people.

Seeing these things, Matilda lifted herself up on the tips of her big toes, big and bashful as box turtles, and let herself go. She felt as if she were falling, but her feet dangled beneath her as she rose. The skyscraper ascended to such an altitude that beyond the fifty-third floor it disappeared into the invisible blue that loomed above it, and its existence became more a matter of divination and faith. Matilda, who so longed to be a believer, wondered how long it would take for her to reach the top. She thought of faithful people stepping into an elevator and taking it to a floor that might be no more than rumor, the door opening onto sky, and she felt her heart stutter in her chest. The girl was rising.

Matilda had risen into the early evening and the moon, an eager spectator of a defiant physics, leapt into the sky so quickly, it nearly fumbled all its belongings and collided with the sun, and the two lights spreading across the ambivalent sky briefly illuminated all the rasping bones animating the universe, hobbled recently by lumbago. Matilda looked down at her irradiated interior and saw clearly this rising would come at a cost. She was glad she had eaten dessert.

At this uncertain hour on the cusp of evening, the terraces and balconies were filled with people whose hands were obsolete, yet they continued to use them, to hold forks, to button and unbutton shirts, to signal to the hard-of-hearing maître d' how many people were in their party. In this way, the hands persuaded themselves they were relevant. Matilda rose and the hands of people reached out but could not grasp her feet, ungainly spoonbills paddling the air, so waved instead, then returned themselves to the loose flesh pooling at their owners' throats.

This was the only skyscraper in Kansas, where levitation was exceedingly rare, but when it did happen, the surrounding plains filled with the following: Indians slain by colonial microbes, in search of youth and gold, and settlers done in by a first winter's unmerciful meteorology; feedlots full of narrowly caged cows thickening, thickening; overturned stagecoaches bleeding goldbricks and barrels of gunpowder; saloons noisy with the flaring tempers of gunslingers and the sound of tables being pounded by the patsies of cardsharps; crusaders of the Women's Temperance Union brandishing hatchets and swinging at the scalps of barkeeps, singing, *Good morning, apocalypse! Salutations, destroyer of men's souls!*; foreclosed-upon farm widows, fretful neurasthenics, made tranquil and amnesiac by a snifter of laudanum of an evening; sex-scandaled preachers and pregnant salutatorians and women made breathless by whalebone corsets; farm machine amputees and once-golden quarterbacks, both feeding their paunch with Wild Turkey and spitting tobacco into a Dairy Maid cup. All raised their hands optimistically toward the riser, hosanna! When someone rose above the flattened earth, it was a hopeful time in Kansas.

The sun, so self-conscious at this time of day, could not help but toss an unraveling skein of light toward Matilda, prone to chill, and she wrapped it about her like a cardigan sweater. She knew a roseate glow only improves a girl's prospects.

Matilda felt tears on her cheeks, though her ducts had long ago left her for a more sorrowful face, and then she saw the silken droplets of an opulent serein falling around her, such a promising shade of green, and it looked like tiny katydids were dropping from the sky and alighting on the tip of her nose, her lips, her outstretched arms greening!

There were many men on the balconies who had money in bloated sacks spilling over the arms of the chairs in their living rooms, and these men, wanting to attract Matilda's attention, shed their overalls and flannel shirts and the ball caps that hid their secretly twinkling cue balls beneath, and they slid into long-tailed tuxedoes and stovepipe hats, and they held out to Matilda a fistful of jewels, a handsome cast-iron skillet, and a bolt of gingham. "Dear winsome prairie dog," they sang, "lovely little cotton rat, fond darting pipistrelle, fatal armadillo, sturdy vertebrate, goddess of diversified teeth, hand us your four-chambered heart, to whose perfect cadence we can easily waltz, heave the honeysuckled breath from your ample mammalian diaphragm, dear bobcatwapitioppossum, come canoodle with us!" These were men of significant sugar, and they fluttered their useless hands in front of her rising eyes on the chance that those dreamy peepers might be vulnerable to mesmerism.

"I am sorry, rich barons of Kansas," said Matilda, "but what hovering enchantress worth her girth can be as easily won as that?" and she plucked a hair from the beard of the hoariest among them. Matilda had studied the Great Kansas Rising of 1913 and knew it was important not to slow her velocity for a tryst with a terrace libertine, however tempting his ballroom duds. Then she thought of her father, earnest as an ear of corn, arms tan to the elbow, duck-down hair slicked with scented oil, frying mush or pouring batter onto the waffle iron of a Sunday morning, dead three years now, and she missed him.

Men of means by the balconyful were captivated by her, by Matilda, the most buoyant girl-colossus in Kansas, and this filled her with the satisfying sensation of having eaten a raw steak, maybe two: Matilda felt substantial. She wanted to stop and relish the attention, but when a corn-fed midwestern girl, big-boned girl weighted down by a lifetime of second helpings of scalloped potatoes and apple brown betty, begins to rise, well, there's no slowing that blithe zeppelin! Matilda's heart and liver were shrugging off gravity at a faster clip than the rest of her, squeezing through the narrow channel of her throat, rising inside her skull, pressing against her optic nerves, blurring her vision, elbowing her brain to the side, her head growing fat with heart, so she gave her arms a robust flap to catch up to her most exuberant parts, parts she did not want to have to try to do without, though she knew many people who had, a great many hearts and livers and kidneys abandoned every day on the side of the road. People saw the various organs that littered the ditches but pretended they did not, and later called the liver collector to discreetly dispose of them. When she was young, she had helped her uncle, the taxidermist, gather castoffs on weekends, and the first heart she found, no bigger than a plum, still sat in a White Owl cigar box atop her dresser, next to the tortoiseshell hair combs her grandmother had given her. Matilda was sixteen and not yet married.

Though Matilda had been rising like a yeasty loaf for hours now, passing floor upon floor of admiring men, the building's apogee seemed no nearer. The prairie had finally taken the sun hostage, as it did every night in Kansas. The moon objected halfheartedly then rose to its perch.

The sun shone so selectively, thought Matilda, making these lives temperate and pleasant, these languid and difficult, incubating disease in others. Of course the moon was no great shakes either with all its tidal and menstrual manipulations. Really she couldn't say which orb nettled her less. In any case, Matilda felt it was not her place, as a rising Kansas girl and a tall drink of water, to feel strongly one way or the other about such matters.

Now Matilda no longer saw only groups of well-heeled men inside the skyscraper. She saw a gathering of infuriated soybeans and green corn debating heatedly the extinction of their race, the genetically modified among them hanging their heads as they sobbed their stories and pounded the lectern. How they longed for the bygone days of detasseling! Suicide seeds leapt from windows to their deaths, and it looked to Matilda as though the building were weeping, or sowing itself into the landscape below, next year's skyscraper sterile as a minute to midnight.

And she saw women sipping water from a calabash at the end of a blistering August, midwifing horses as they foaled, and churning butter wearily with milk already gone to clabber; thinning wet nurses with greedy infants affixed to their breasts, all but drunk dry; ashen women ignoring ailments so that they might meet the Great Physician sooner; stenographers grown nearly deaf from taking endless dictation at all hours of the night. Matilda's mother had urged her to learn to play the accordion, so that she would always have something to fall back on, and though she hoped she would never have occasion to return to Kansas (at least not without a sequined ball gown, a means of conveyance that cost a pretty penny, and an extravagantly mustachioed man on her arm), she was glad she knew how to carry a jaunty tune. She imagined such a skill might prove invaluable at this height.

But it was that roomful of babies that gave Matilda the howling jimjams. Babies crawling on every surface, spitting up strained peas with an air of squalling entitlement, babies with fists full of somebody's hair, babies that shrieked at a pitch that made all the windows in the skyscraper tremble. Then one baby, plump as a partridge, crawled onto the wall of the balcony, and Matilda knew she should nudge it back to safety with her little finger, but she was curious to know what would happen to so fat a baby should it toss itself into the breach. She could already see from its chubby little downturned scowl she was a great disappointment to this baby, and she wished it would stop drooling so accusingly and return to the mewling herd. Matilda had always found babies with their crusted noses and defenseless fontanelles and legs like dinner rolls *deeply* unsettling. This one was no exception: sticky, spooky, slobbering moppet.

As Matilda continued to ascend, dogs and cats gathered in the moonlight and sat on their haunches, draped themselves across deck chairs, eyeing her appraisingly. The dogs, faithful guardians of front doors, believed nevertheless it was not their job to warn the night sky of a possible prowler, so they kept their muzzles buttoned, chewed their paws and sneezed. The cats, boozy with cream, made half-hearted swats at Matilda's jouncing braids, which reminded them of mice scattering.

The night air was bracing, and Matilda shuddered with gooseflesh. Some of the people who lived farther up, on the late-night floors, people who had clearly seen this sort of thing before and so knew how to properly respond, appeared on their balconies and offered her a wrap and a mug of buttered rum, but Matilda was a large and graceless girl, and each thing she reached for disappeared through her bumbling fingers. "Forgive me!" called Matilda, "I have never risen before and cannot slow my rising, but I will tell the people above of your kindness," and these people with extra sweaters collected and stored in cedar closets in preparation for just this occasion tendered her their most parental smiles.

Looking upward, Matilda thought she saw now the lights of the penthouse flickering into view. She saw two-seater dirigibles and aerodynamic velocipedes being handed over to the sky's valet, and she watched as people who lived so far from Kansas strode brightly across the sky like comets and disappeared into the glittering night. Such effortless people living so far above the tree line, which was already so far above Kansas, she never knew! A velvety snow began to fall on the moon, now a-snooze. This must be, thought Matilda, where heads of state go to celebrate the armistice of impulsive wars their hearts had never been in. She had always wanted to have a reason to deny her appetite for the sake of her country, to show her fortitude on meatless days, rationing her capacious hunger. She had a jar at home where she stored rendered fats, ready to extract glycerin for the war effort should gunpowder be again suddenly in demand. Matilda knew how to be resourceful, how to stockpile things of which there would one day no longer be a surplus, things like river rocks and rubber tires and the hollow bones of cardinals. The world would come to her when they were gone. She had a clement disposition. Like Job she knew how to weather the most capricious infirmity, had borne a carbuncle or two with equanimity and a little salve. She knew how to shoe a recalcitrant horse.

Only days ago had Matilda sat on her stool yanking the shriveled udders of their elderly cow, who dispensed now only dust, and Matilda dreamt of rising into a glamorous fate such as this one, a night bejeweled with the beautifully capped teeth of the people who had been inoculated against the wasting disease of Kansas, a malady she herself was determined to recover from if she had to sacrifice every last 4-H ribbon and prizewinning Jersey Wooly and Flemish Giant and Blue of Ham to do so!

But just as Matilda passed the 364th floor, she saw below her a speck of light, absurd in its defiant faintness, like a flashlight trained on a star many light years its senior, a light that seemed to spring from the ground, which was now, to Matilda's delight, only hearsay. At first she couldn't tell if it was rising or falling, and then it started to take shape, and Matilda could see . . . what? could see . . . wait, why it looked like . . . it was! another girl on the rise!

The girl wore a gold lamé pencil dress that made her look to Matilda like a glistering fish leaping in firelight, and she cuddled with a mink stole, a pouty little bee-stung grin pursed beneath her button nose. Her silver shoes competed with the moonlight, and she trailed a cloud of enchanted moths looping crazily behind her. When she reached Matilda's feet, Matilda extended to this girl her hand, big and bright as a Mediterranean noon, and she felt as though she were offering this blazing girl something a little unseemly in its excess, something like, say, Neptune, an impractical gratuity (*really, it was too much, she was merely doing her job and hadn't the least expectation of being so handsomely compensated for her trouble, and anyway how could she possibly care for such a spirited and demanding planet, in whose paddock would she board it?*), but the girl just licked her rutilant lips, red as pimiento, and gave her hand a limp toss, and though it took her some minutes to travel the three stories of Matilda, she eventually passed her by, and now she made Matilda think of those ambitious bubbles effervescing toward their death in a flute of champagne. Matilda so wished she'd thought to cream her elbows.

And then Matilda saw that there were others: girls in hoopskirts floating upward like umbrellas eternally opening; girls in saddle shoes with pom-poms exploding above their heads like sparklers; girls holding platters of corned beef and cabbage and grinning into the flashbulb of a dyspeptic moon; girls whose long legs served as a monthly tourniquet as they crossed them in midair to stanch the blood that would soon soak through to their white gym shorts; girls who looked like the most ravishing rabbits as they bounded across the night; girls to whom, without their glasses, the sky appeared to be filled with polished nickels; girls who wore long sleeves to hide the white scars on their forearms resulting from the long-ago nip of a cranky dachshund; girls with just-washed hair the color of river water at night; all the girls so smartly proportioned. These girls were delicious! And Matilda suddenly wanted to eat them after tenderizing them with a mallet. Well, no, she supposed that wasn't exactly right. She often looked at people and saw T-bones or cheesecake or buttered biscuits. Matilda wished there had been more opportunities to do calisthenics in the crisp morning air with other girls like her, girls soon to rise, long, sturdy girls, winsome as a field of winter wheat, lonely monadnocks who'd been rising up from the plains of Kansas their whole lives.

Despite a strange tingling behind her knees, Matilda now felt abstract, like an idea so impenetrable it would instantly render the thinker unconscious, and the moon, preoccupied with the sun's capture, with foreign relations it had meant to mend and the certainty that it would lose to the incumbent come morning, lent her no guidance.

All the lights the skyscraper uttered now began to dim, the balconies she passed mostly vacant, only disconsolate potted plants extending their shriveled fronds to her. The building continued to rise alongside her, but the moon appeared to voluntarily impale itself on a crowning spire and then the glow at the top turned wispily to smoke like a candle dampened.

Matilda was seized by a terrifying thought: what if at the building's unimaginably fetching zenith she were to find nothing but . . . Kansas? She felt a tightening in her chest, as though her heart had squeezed into a wasp-waisted dress two sizes too small. Sometimes Matilda fantasized about throttling her own heart and leaving it for dead at the side of the road for her uncle to find and stuff, but she knew her heart trusted her, and she had so long been its custodian that she couldn't quite bring herself to betray its dependence upon her, however merely habitual.

Once when Matilda was spinning a globe dreamily, fingering exotic locales surrounded by silver water and the pink light of unending summer, her grandmother said, "There are worse things than Kansas," and when Matilda asked what they were, her grandmother took her by the hand, led her outside, pointed at the incandescent night, and said, "There are places in the world where the dead are sold for kindling." She told Matilda that Jesus was schooled in raising the dead and he knew how to triage, knew which dearly departed were resurrectable and which just had to stay dead. "But," said her grandmother, "when you raise the dead here on earth, they only fall back down to die again. Hardly worth the trouble," and she went back inside to jaw a bit before bed, as she did every night, with her dead husband's picture.

And then there her grandmother suddenly was, dead five years herself but lilting toward Matilda, looking no worse for wear, rising, rising.

Or was she falling? Matilda was close enough now to see that her grandmother's housecoat hung on her like a handkerchief caught on a sapling, the flesh of her calves drooping around her ankles like sagging socks, but fire encircled her leathery face, a stunning mane of flames that brought out the once-fertile green of her eyes, and then Matilda realized her grandmother must have come from above, from the place toward which she herself was now traveling, and at the periphery of Matilda's vision a moving picture began to sharpen: a picture of her mother sitting in the cellar next to mason jars full of corn relish and pickled okra and weeping into her blistered hands, a picture of a second sun erupting over the horizon like a scalding flower unfolding, of creeping people with molten skin flowing down their bones, fallen cows lying scattered beneath dejected willows, fish dazzling as detonation floating against the current in a reddened river, the slender ghosts of children hidden in caves awaiting the piper's return, the wan moon whiskered with light, surrendering as it hurtled toward tomorrow. And Matilda saw herself rocketing toward the pale stars of a dimming Andromeda, rising toward the catastrophe of morning, saw herself let go of the night, while the sun's parishioners far below opened windows and doors to see a thousand risen Lazaruses falling over Kansas.

FAUNA

Animalmancy

after Italo Calvino

Once there was a well-heeled ventriloquist who, before being escorted out on a rail, made a killing in Vegas with a stage show in which he sat the Recently Dead on his knee and manually reanimated them. He did this so as to channel and pass along the Deceased's final fond regards to those Dearly Beloved who had schlepped their remains across ocean and dale for this parting communiqué. This man, a widower, had a son name of Busby with a reedy voice like a far-off clarinet and a brain so gymnastic he could look at the sky and accurately predict the next three things that would appear there: orphaned goose, traffic 'copter, sizzling rain that could disfigure a face. Eventually Nikolai, Busby's father, *aerosaltant of the voice* is how he thought of himself as he snapped his suspenders, got the bum's rush in Vegas when an angry wife brought charges against him for impersonation of the Dead, defamation of a grieving widow, and unlawful ventriloquism (there are a lot of things you can throw in Las Vegas—the dice, a fight, your weight around—but not a voice). The widow's outrage had burst into being when the husband's teeth clack-clack-clacked with what seemed like recovered longing. He spoke wistfully of the lovely long-ago days of the courtship of his wife, whom he said had been beautiful. *As beautiful as . . . the chapped and empurpled ass of a mandrill!* sputtered Nikolai, mere messenger, and then he inhaled quickly, as though he might be able to suck the words out of the air and back into his lungs again before they reached the ears of the wife. The man's wife looked up from her sodden handkerchief, and narrowed her eyes, and out of a mouth that looked like it lunched regularly on lemons came a shriek. She yowled, at a piercing decibel, that Nikolai was a fraud and insisted he be taken away in manacles. But what most infuriated the widow was not the unflattering comparison, which was in fact the sort of elaborate barb the husband was known for, but the word "beautiful," an adjective the woman's husband had never in his life used to describe her, and she believed it was all the unlikelier that he would do so in death. What you get, thought Nikolai, for trying to soften the vituperations of the Dead, who can be full of vinegar in those first days following their departure, especially those who are reluctant to relax their claws, let go of the perch, and fall to the be-schmutzed newspaper beneath. Nikolai's mouth often tasted of pickled eggs after a performance, and he'd once thought he might cheer up a somber audience by releasing a bevy of doves, doves that would rise like a puff of eager wood smoke and settle in the rafters. But then he'd priced a passel of discount doves from a wholesaler in Sparks and decided solemnity was what was called for after a loved one belches his last.

So Nikolai, thinking he wanted for his Busby a life less vulnerable to the charge of felonious entertainments, secured the services of an omnilingual tutor, so that Busby could learn to converse with the Dead in any language. Upon mastering 332 tongues, including Míkmawísimk, Airedale Terrier, Godoberi, Chickasaw, Cormorant, Slime Mold, Uzbek, Musk Ox, Fiddlehead Fern, Hungarian, and !Kung, Busby returned home to his father, and the twittering music that spilled from his lips throughout his dreaming was so enchanting it caused the birds that crowded the loblolly pine outside his window to shirk their matutinal duties and snooze until noon. His father knew only that he'd become fluent in Hindi and Mandarin, languages spoken in locales where he believed the Dead might not remain as indisputably dead and dumb as they do in Nevada, and he saw far-flung travel opportunities and finely tailored gold lamé suit jackets in their future.

One summer evening, with Busby home and freshly graduated, father and son strolled through a park near their house, Nikolai throwing his voice punitively into any be-poodled passerby that refused to nod hello: *My father thought me an inchworm, a quarter inchworm, even less!*; *My wife slaps me as I sleep and longs to tug the beats from my heart until it stops*; *I am destitute and all alone with less than a teaspoon of jam in the jar and moths gnawing at my pockets*; *I fed my daughter, wan as a turnip, the wrong physic for her illness, and she turned to boiled water in my hands*; *When I step from my door, the sky empties of birds and the light grows dull as dread*; *I have never eased the suffering of another, will leave the world a far duskier place than I found it*, moaned the air beside these people as they scuttled past Nikolai, yanking their mutts behind them.

And then as the seventeen-year cicadas sawed hypnotically, the swelling sound, loud and symphonic, caused Busby's father to fall to the ground, cover his head with his arms, and prepare for the blitz, which never came. "Those wretched little chainsaws!" growled his father. "Always chewing at my ears!"

"May I translate? Would you like to know what the magicicadas are lamenting?" asked Busby.

His father glared at him through the slits of his incredulous eyes and said, "What would you know of the lamentation of insects? What entomological hocus-pocus do you believe yourself to be schooled in? Remember, when it comes to the well-spoken speechless, I wrote the book!"

Busby smiled, for he had read his father's book, *Unlocking the Lips of the Newly Dead: Necrolinguistics Made Easy*, and found it wanting in precisely the area of animal communication.

As they strolled farther, an argumentative jay began to follow them and prattled a blue streak behind them. Nikolai's eyes narrowed at Busby beneath a woolen V of pinched eyebrows, and he braced himself for the insufferable utterance he knew would follow.

"Would you—"

"No!" boomed the father.

In the distance, a huddle of llamas were yawping and spitting and pricking up their ears skeptically as llamas do, and Busby stifled a snort. His father turned on him and roared, "What have I spent my hard-earned, carefully stockpiled cabbage on? Have I been nearly tarred and feathered in the best casinos in the country for this? There is no wisdom what passes from birdly beak to human ear! Did your charlatan teacher school you in Ignoramus? Did he teach you to dissertate in Dodo?" His father growled and his upper lip shivered like the withers of a horse, "Prrrrpf! Work of the Devil," he said, then added, "I suppose you speak that too!"

Busby's teacher had warned him there were those in the world whose ears would never acknowledge the great din of animal gabble that filled the air. You had only to tune your ears to the correct frequencies, but few had the gift for doing so. Busby's ears swiveled fractions of degrees to pick up the transmissions, a precise auditory calibration the key to an accurate translation. He had imagined his father would be happy at the thought of the new service he might add to the menu of his bereavement offerings. Think of it, in death, a malamute, an Abyssinian cat, a potbellied pig might finally feel free to hold forth and express their earthly devotion to or share their innermost yearnings with their grieving owners. And those notoriously devoted ferret fanciers! Surely they were in need and deserving of consolation too. (The logorrhea of ferrets made them a formidable challenge to translate, but they spoke in a clever, if chatterbox, idiom, and Busby found them edifying and well worth the labor.) His father could hold the beloved Puccini or Fraulein or Opposable Thumb or Socrates or Lymph Node or Fairy Dust or Lawn Dart or Mutt-Mutt in his arms and snap its tiny muzzle as Busby and his father spoke in unison, Nikolai channeling the death song, Busby the animal soul, snappity-snap-snap. Busby had long dreamt of the moment, but it was now clear his father would never consent to partnering in such a business, and this made Busby feel suddenly dejected and without words.

Nikolai spent the night pacing about in his study, wringing his hands, trying to decide what to do about his son, who might well be demoniacal and beyond exorcising. Busby's mother had been a pious woman who campaigned for the vindication of the rights of the Dead, whom she believed were treated shabbily, stored in dark, squalid places, robbed of all belongings, unfed, unspoken to, looked upon as little more than a pile of old bones that made no worthwhile contribution, forgotten. The Dead, she believed, moldered on principle, a symptom of exile.

She died from a sudden fever when Busby was just a young boy at the stumbling beginnings of acquiring complicated speech, and when he looked upon his mother's newly unbreathing face, scrubbed clean and colorless as a parsnip, he put his ear to her mouth. "Always speak the truth," she whispered, "even in death, love the Dead who came before you, and give the unemancipated their due—their day will come, dear busy-boy Busby, busy as a B." Busby straightened up with a start. It was his father's raspy voice. He stood in the doorway, and his mouth looked like a wounded animal rising shakily to its hooves as his lips shaped themselves into a faint smile. He had loved her with the dissolving desperation that the setting sun loves nightfall. Busby could see this in the way his father's once-polished eyes now appeared be-grimed with grief.

Some hours after, as Nikolai sat beside his wife and looked out the window at the hayfield fluttering in the sunlight, Violet sat up in the deathbed, creakily put her feet to the floor, stood, and began to dismantle herself, unhinging an arm and laying it on the bed; unfastening each vertebral button on her back and slipping out of her skin, which she let fall to the floor; ejecting her eyes and depositing them in the dish of her husband's cufflinks on the nightstand; then she summoned together what bones remained undiscarded, gathered Nikolai's face into her makeshift hands, and said, *Creature*. She said, *Comely vertebrate*. She said, *A man's heart, a man's body, is no truer than those of a dog, his belly no truer than the four stomachs of a Holstein. Less true, in fact, because a man knows better, knows that even the four footed suffer and grieve, but, for the sake of a Sunday roast and an elevating order, pretends he does not. This knowledge*, said Violet, *is my final gift to you. Dear Nikolai, my beloved, singer of the parting arias of the Dead, I had no choice but to die in order for you to hear me. Pity*, and then she collapsed to ash. Nikolai took to his bed and sobbed into his nightshirt and silently swore off all matters zoological as well as the feral truths that had left him a widower and his boy half orphaned.

And then, like the fist of a disgruntled widow's brawny son, it struck him: perhaps if Busby were no longer among the Living, Nikolai might be able to better understand him, might be able to communicate with his son, with whom he had spoken so little over the years. And he imagined, too, that his dear Violet, Busby's mother, would be overjoyed (the Dead, stoic to beat the band, often appeared underjoyed, but Nikolai knew this was only their attempt to meet the expectations of the Living) to see her boy again after all these years. Perhaps the three of them might even have a family colloquy, with Busby, who would be newly departed, acting as interpreter for the Distant Dead, his mother, who had once been very communicative but was now a voice that only occasionally fluttered the front curtains, rattling the rusting padlock on Nikolai's long-shackled heart.

So Nikolai rang up Messrs. Guernsey and Clydesdale, gentlemen he'd had occasion to meet in Vegas, when they mistook him for a grifting gambler on whom they'd been hired to put the squeeze. It seemed that Nikolai, who compulsively stroked his Vandyke and occasionally donned a monocle purely for show, was a dead ringer for a deadbeat that their boss, a notoriously impatient and usurious casino owner, wished to force, by way of a broken wing or two, to straighten up and fly right, Nikolai's feckless doppelgänger having accrued a sizable debt that ballooned with every passing minute's compounding-compounding interest. Before officially roughing him up, they dumped Nikolai at the feet of their employer, who took one glare at him and roared that they'd pinched the wrong mope. They apologized and promised Nikolai one free leg-breaking for his trouble, should he ever find himself in need of their specialized services. Nikolai called in that marker and explained the service he was seeking, and that night the wolves came scratching at Busby's door.

Mr. Guernsey and Mr. Clydesdale, standing before him with professional erectness, told Busby his father had asked them to escort him to the morgue, where Nikolai would meet Busby and begin to instruct him in the embittered blather of the Recently Deceased. Busby, a trusting fellow, whose niggling suspicions of the motives of others usually remained fallow, climbed into the back of the black sedan and seated himself next to a white dog be-stippled with black spots and bearing a head like an anvil and a flaring snout that was an unseemly pink. The dog's tongue hung out of his mouth like a spent party favor, and then a low rumbling issued from deep in his burly breast. The dog sniffed the air and emitted two curtailed barks, then lay down and lowered his flat head between his paws.

Busby was unable to stifle a gasp, for the dog had just tipped him to the true meaning of this euphemistic "trip to the morgue." Busby whined quietly, and the dog, whose name was Gerald, though the two mugs insisted on calling him Incisor, explained to Busby how he had been dragged, against his well-muscled will, into this life of criminality. He had once been an upstanding canine, a cadaver dog employed by Johnny Law to sniff out the decomposing flesh of ousted mafiosi on the brink of incriminating testimony and a life of witness protection ("*witless* protection if you ask me," sniffed Gerald), straight through the foundations of the recently erected buildings in which these recovering mobsters frequently wound up. And then one night Gerald's precinct was stormed, and Mr. Guernsey appeared at his kennel waving a pork chop under his schnoz (feeding time had come and gone with nary a kibble and so he was weaker willed than usual). Then he pushed Gerald into a tight-fitting harness that permitted only modest breathing and on into a crate that smelled distinctly and offensively feline, like a dissipated Persian, the nerve. And since that day, Mutt and Mutt, as Gerald liked to call them, had used him as backup and as a silent spectator to their thuggery, forcing him to witness the other side of cadaver-hood, those awful minutes before.

Upon hearing this last conspiratorial snarl, Mr. Clydesdale turned around and filliped Gerald on the muzzle. "All right now. He ain't goin' nowhere. Give it a rest, 'Cisor." He turned and grinned a solicitous gold-capped grin at Busby and said, "His bark is, you know, heh." Oh, Busby knew. He smiled.

Gerald said, *Psst. At the next stoplight, I'll chomp on that nape, the delectable color of schmaltz, hovering above the headrest*—he paused to salivate; dogs, as Busby well knew, were extremely distractible creatures, with a loping hither-and-thither sense of conversation, forever treeing squirrels in their imaginations—*and you make a break for it.* And then Gerald said, *Shake,* and he and Busby both waggled their behinds and guffawed silently. At the next stoplight, Gerald did as he said and sank his choppers into Mr. Guernsey's withers. Busby jumped out as pandemonium ensued inside the sedan, and he ran and flagged down a crosstown bus and hopped inside.

Only then did it begin to fully dawn on Busby that there was a bounty on his head, one bankrolled by his father, that . . . that . . . sideshow necromancer! But he couldn't sustain his outrage for long, and he looked out the window and understood as he watched the spire of a boarded-up cathedral impale the sagging sun that there was no creature in the world to whom he could communicate his sorrow.

Meanwhile, Nikolai wore a groove in the hearth as he paced fretfully in front of the fireplace and stared at its dying embers. He pleaded with Violet's picture, hanging above the mantel, to stir the ashes and tell him he had been right to want to reunite the family in this way and to prevent Busby from living a laughable life, but the ashes remained unmoved. Nikolai understood divination from the Dead could only tell you what you already knew, but he had always relied on Violet to reassure him that what he knew was indeed worth knowing, however much that knowledge made him vulnerable to the sodden heckling of intoxicated conventioneers.

The only person Busby could think of to turn to for help was Mr. Vulpecula, his polyglot tutor. The instant Mr. Vulpecula opened the door, Busby felt relief erupt in him like a glottal plosive, and he smiled gratefully at Mr. Vulpecula's persimmon-colored hair, the slightly steepled ears that needed tweezing, and the long and handsome nose that made him look both compliant and clever. "Dear boy, dear boy!" exclaimed Mr. Vulpecula, shaking his head as he listened to Busby's tale, and then he visibly beamed when Busby recounted his conversation with Gerald.

They waited until night was full upon them, and then Mr. Vulpecula drove Busby to that ramshackle church he had seen earlier, and inside they were met by five members of a local chapter of PETAL, People for the Ethical Treatment of Animal Linguists. Mr. Vulpecula had himself been a charter member, but he'd developed a sensitivity to the smell of formaldehyde, and this kept him from sneaking late at night into laboratories to liberate the linguists incarcerated there in cages, electrodes dotting their sallow bodies, wood shavings sticking to their cheeks, a spigot that curved through the bars dripping drugged water that anaesthetized in them any ambition to flee. There was money to be made and wars to be won by intel gathered from far-flung fauna, but most animal linguists, a loyal lot, kept their traps snapped and muttered a glossolalia that caused the cryptography machines to emit smoke and hum to silence.

Unfortunately, Messrs. Guernsey and Clydesdale, smarter than they looked, anticipating Busby would seek refuge here, lay in wait. They leapt in front of him and barred his entrance into the church sanctuary, dragging poor Gerald whining behind them on a devilishly pronged choke chain. But the PETALers were ready for the kerfuffle that followed, and they knocked the brutes to the ground, giving Busby the opportunity to scram yet again. As Busby broke free, he told the thugs that if they informed his father the deed was done, he'd disappear and his father would be no wiser. For a brief instance, Busby was hopeful this *mishigas* might somehow work itself out, but then he looked back to see Mr. Vulpecula dabbing Gerald's injured throat with a handkerchief and quietly howling into his other hand.

This time, Busby fled to the woods, where he had spent the long and lonely days during his mother's waning. There he came upon a brightly scummed pond and heard two frogs bickering in the midnight slant of moonlight, as frogs everywhere are wont to do. This was a dialect of bullfrog unfamiliar to Busby, and he could not quite decipher the gist of the argument, but he heard one frog croak, *Body of Christ! Body of Christ!* to which the other responded, *Well, Mr.*

High Priest of the Small Pond, are we? and she belched scornfully. *Come, fumblefingers, stop being such a polliwog! Toss me the Host-in-Training else I'm out of this puddle! Come now, the Body, we've kept it whole this long. Say now, give it a toss, lovey. Time to bury it, so little girl can commune in the afterpond, she can.*

Busby drew closer to the pond and in the light silvering the speckled skin, he could see the frogs were playing ball with a mummified fly pinned to a tiny cross, bearing a striking resemblance to . . . oh my! Busby gasped and the frogs turned their bulging headlights on him and gulped. *Pardon me*, croaked Busby, though he feared he might accidentally have said, *pity me*, and one of the frogs nodded and said, *Little girl she died.* And the other frog hung her head and said, *Hid the consecrated host* (words here he couldn't decode, a peeling eeeeerpf) *under tongue—very hungry was she very hungry and found herself craving heart-soul-and-soup-bone the body of Christ, but didn't feel it a proper appetite, did she, so she spit it in the pond and . . . ate-it-we-ate-it! Ate-it-we-ate-it!* they chorused. *Little girl she died. Been working on resurrection ever since*, said the other frog, *or at least amends*, who ballooned his handsome throat apologetically. *Buried yonder she is*, said the other, and she snapped her tongue in the direction of a clearing where a lonely tombstone tilted.

Busby stood over the grave of the little girl and heard a distant mewling, which he recognized: it was a sound he'd heard as a child when he visited his mother in the cemetery, a sobbing sound like shrill rain-swept wind beating against a curtain through an open window.

A farmer, face furrowed with sorrow, appeared, and he stopped his ritual wandering when he saw Busby. "What business," asked the farmer, "have you here, sir, at the gravesite of my daughter?"

"Your daughter," said Busby, "she took to her bed one Sunday, wasted away for weeks, unable to bear the sight of food: she thought it better to starve herself than partake of Christ when ravenous (as that had already been done and to devastating outcome)."

At this the farmer whitened, and he demanded to know who Busby was and whence he'd gathered this intelligence.

Busby cast his eyes in the direction of the pond and settled on the two frogs, who sat side-by-side blinking and burping in the moonlight. "I know someone," he said, "who could help you," and he gave the farmer his father's card and told him to say fellow name of Busby had recommended him. The frogs sidled up next to them, and the four of them stood looking at the grave of the farmer's daughter, each one considering the cruel consequences that befell a bravely starving soul when it refused that complicated nourishment that demands a body sate itself with suffering. *Can't beat the Reaper*, yodeled one frog. *World is mortal and fleeting as a shadfly*, chirruped the other, and the moon tumbled behind the trees and the sky darkened in agreement.

Nikolai felt low, lower than the crumbling backside of a buried man, man felled by deadly contagion and therefore dusted with quicklime and stashed deep in the bubonic earth. Yes, Nikolai felt low, unsure now if his parental and familial instincts had been the right ones. When Hoodlum Clydesdale appeared at his door to tell him it was a done deed, a "*fate* accompli," Nikolai, who couldn't help but peer into the lives of the Dead hovering around all people with whom he had any dealings, informed this halter of men's hearts that his mother had whinnied regretfully at the scraggly sight of his then re-cently fetal self, for she knew he would never clip-clop at the front of a parade or canter with the show ponies. Mr. Clydesdale, feeling in his own shrunken heart the painful truth of the claim, which had been the likely reason beneath his turning to a life of iniquity, snif-fled and shuffled backward out the door, his felonious ham fists stuffed in his pockets.

So when the farmer begged Nikolai to help him communicate with his daughter, Nikolai was so leaden with grief, he was scarcely able to hold himself upright, but the farmer was insistent, and when he told Nikolai it was Busby who had given him his name, Busby's father was helpless to resist his appeal.

Nikolai stood at the headstone of the grave of the farmer's daughter, upon which sat two snoring bullfrogs, bags under their bulging eyes, clearly pooped from a long night of croaking at the moon. And he tried hard to get a fix on the sound of the girl's soul, invited her to speak to her woebegone father, but he could only hear a high-pitched wind whistling past his ears. Finally, he got a lock on a staticky frequency that eventually cleared and, on the breeze of an exhalation, said, *Always speak the truth, even in death, love the Dead who came before you, and give the unemancipated their due, dear knick-knack Nikolai-alkali-can-tell-no-lie.* And at this, Nikolai's heart thudded to a halt in his chest and he crumpled to his knees.

At that moment, as the green light of the world eddied around him, Nikolai saw Violet and a little girl in a tattered dress sit up and dust the dirt from their faces, and they tugged on Nikolai's beard and laughed and keened and leapt into the wind, and he heard one bullfrog belch to the other, *She's risen, she is!* And as Nikolai sank into the soil, he trembled at the thought of the conversation he could finally have with his Violet now that they were both dead, neither needing to animate the other, and he saw his son's face, his radiant, milk-fed, unmurdered face, saw Busby's mouth undulating above him like a field of timothy seen from a window, and he heard a distant barking then a baying then a mewling then a clucking, and Busby's lips slowed their flutter. Nikolai felt his own mammalian blood slowing to a creep, soon to loiter in his veins, and the truth of it all gripped him by the gullet as he felt his breast bloat into marsupium, his feet split into hooves, his fingers web, his stomach quarter itself: rumen, reticulum, omasum, abomasum, felt his bones empty as bones do when the Dead ready themselves for flight.

The Girl, the Wolf, the Crone

More than once there was a soon-to-be-old woman who had a loaf of bread, held it in her hands she did, and it was inconvenient to have a loaf of bread always sitting in her hands as she tried to sweep or sew or sneeze, so she said to her daughter, the one with cheeks the appalling color of let blood: "With a face like that, you haven't anything better to do, so here, take this bread off my hands!" The woman said she knew a sickly wolf who would like nothing better than to receive stale bread from a girl like her, "but be careful," said the girl's mother, "as the woods are full of primordial women with faces like the bottom of a river and who long to feel the weight of bread in their twisted mitts once more." The minute the woman handed the bread to the girl, her face grew dark as thunder, and she barked, "Git!"

The girl fled with the loaf under her arm and at the fork where everyone chooses wrongly, she saw a crusty old woman with a face like a fallen cake, and the woman yowled, "You're headed the wrong way, dear heart!"

"But I haven't chosen yet!" said the girl with the objectionable cheeks.

"As if that mattered," muttered the woman, and for a moment her face looked like a weathered map leading nowhere good.

The girl examined the tines of the forking path and could see that in one direction the road was covered in spoons and in the other it was littered with blood sausages. The girl had always preferred spoon to sausage, and so she confidently strode in that direction. The sunlight that needled its way through the branches of the forest struck the bowed bellies of the spoons, splintered in every direction, and pricked the girl's skin as she walked. She tried to brush away the light that beetled along her arms and up her throat with its sticky legs. The light, pragmatic and cowardly at heart, would not go near those cheeks red as a carbuncle.

The old woman, knowing what was expected of her, cackled. She swiftly slipped and wobbled atop the sausages and cursed herself for having forgotten to bring along a growler of beer. No matter, she'd be at the house of the ailing wolf soon enough, and then she'd have her fill, boy howdy.

When she reached the house of the wolf, the cunning beldam let herself in and shook her head at the sight of him: he looked half dead already, more moth-eaten pelt than glamorous savage, not even fit to be a stole. She spit a bolus of sausage at the foot of his bed. The wolf weakly stirred at the sound.

"Well, I suppose I haven't any choice but to eat you," said the woman.

"I suppose not," said the wolf, who'd had a hunch the saving catholicon of the bread would not make it to him in time. There is no rescuing a wolf, not in this world or any other. He unzipped his coat and dragged his body dutifully into her mouth, and the woman, who found him a little gamey, spit the bones onto the bed.

From inside her belly, the wolf's muffled voice came, *Take, eat,* he said, *this is my body, which is broken for you.*

Such theatrics, heavens to Betsy! thought the old woman, and she socked herself in the stomach and belched. If she ate before sundown, her meals always repeated on her.

The ancienne noblesse began to undress, lace-up peeptoes, garters, support hose, daisied duster, crocheted shrug, ragged bonnet.

A yellow cat lying curled before the hearth unwound himself, sat up, and said, "Get a load of granny's gams, ooh-wee hubba-hubba!" then whistled like a sailor newly on leave.

The ripe old dame, whose sister had a weakness for strays of every stripe, had had her fill of cheeky gibs, and she booted him across the room. Then she stepped inside the wolf skin, which fit a skosh too snugly, and slipped beneath the covers. She struck a wan pose and conjured a pallor that announced she was on the verge of oblivion and should be the recipient of a steady supply of pity and bread and the affection of innocents, and just as she did, Little Miss Red Cheeks knocked at the door.

"Allow me," said the limping tom, who wanted to hotfoot it to a place free of irascible old grimalkins, notorious collectors of the likes of him, and he slid out the door sly as butter.

And there the girl was, laden with spoons she'd collected along the way and a crumbling loaf, eager to be cradled in the hands of a long-fallow hag, under her arm.

"Hello, sick wolf," said the poppy, and she set the spoons and the bread upon the floor.

My soul is exceeding sorrowful, lamented the wolf inside the woman, and she coughed hoarsely and slapped her chest, and the girl said, "What was that?" and the woman replied, "My cold is leaving my snout full," and she coughed again.

"I have bread," said the girl, who blushed brash as an open wound, "bread that has never left the hands of my mother until now, bread that can save you."

I will smite the shepherd and scatter the sheep, said the wolf, and the woman poked herself hard in the gut, and her stomach emitted a feeble growl.

The little radish knew there was no love lost between wolf and sheep, but there wasn't a flock to be found for miles around, and she smiled at him pityingly, thinking some poor creatures are simply doomed by instinct, helpless to hallucinate more reachable goals, slave to implausible diets. She picked up two spoons and began to tap a melody on her knees, which made her legs involuntarily kick.

The woman threw back the covers and exposed more fully her lupine duds.

"My, what big breasts you have!" exclaimed the girl with cheeks like molten embers. She dropped the spoons, which landed with a tympanic plonk upon the pile.

So sad when a girl goes ruddy, thought the woman, tsk.

The old woman adjusted her dugs, which, raised in the wild away from the civilizing influence of brassieres, were a little claustrophobic and so tried to escape the suffocating skin of the wolf. She corralled them and they nickered. "The better to suckle you with, dear heart!" said the woman. Pitiful little strawberry, thought she, whom I might once have been able to save had your mother, grrrr, not pinched the loaf from my withered fingers. It is always advisable to bear in mind that the embezzlement of fertility necessarily exacts a stiff tariff.

"Oh, wolf, what blue hair you have!" said the girl. The old woman had only yesterday been to the beauty parlor and chosen a rinse the color of irises. Sprigs of hair escaped through the wolf's ears, and the woman tried to tuck them back inside.

Behold, he is at hand that doth betray me, croaked the woman's belly. She was having a little trouble restraining her feral anatomy, and she put a hand to her complicated crotch and her be-furred breasts and gave everything a shake and an upward tug. Oof, went her stomach.

"What opposable thumbs you have, wolf!" bleated the girl, who began to fear this blue and breasted creature was not all that he seemed, this womanly wolf that smelled vaguely medicinal, giving off an odor of vitamins, blood, and moldering roses. And thumbs, he smelled of thumbs!

"Oh, wolf!" cried the girl. "Your bones, your bones!" She pointed at the pile. "How can you heave your body from hill to dale without them? How can you properly terrorize woodland creatures with only raggedy fur and a pudding of flesh with which to spook them?" Bones were an essential ingredient of both locomotion and thuggery the girl well knew.

The old woman now saw she'd left the bones in plain view on the bed, an osteological oversight, and she took up the wolf's femurs and drummed on the headboard behind her. "If I carry them with me," said the woman, "they don't poke me as much. And, well, they're, uh, erf, much more percussive when not swimming inside me!" The woman halted the racket and could see she was straining even this rosily jowled gull's willful naïveté, so necessary to the telling of stories and the entrapment of children.

The girl bent to fetch the loaf of bread that she hoped would help provoke the wolf's natural canine vitality, and when she did, she spied beneath the bed the old woman's clothes. She remembered what her mother had told her, and she was relieved at the thought that there was one less old woman in the woods to worry about. She put on the old woman's shift and the old woman's shawl and the old woman's bonnet, and she clomped about in the old woman's shoes, and she pretended to scold invisible children and to dab at imaginary dewlaps with an embroidered hanky that she kept tucked beneath her wristwatch, then she picked up the bread and crawled into bed with the wolf, who seemed to her to suffer from womanhood, the worst of all afflictions, a disease she would likely contract in time, and the wolf, quick as the flick of a lizard's tongue, quick as a badger's dander, swallowed her whole like the meat of an oyster. The old woman felt the satisfied satiety of having dined on bread and girl. The girl shimmied down the throat of the wolf clutching the loaf to her breast, only to meet and be drawn into another throat on her way to the wolf's stomach, and she could see this was not the shriveled throat of a bruised peach past her prime. Only then did she realize she'd been bamboozled and was now curled inside the true wolf's boneless belly as if waiting to be born, half wood-sprite-battle-ax, half consumptive cur, nuts! She heard the old woman licking her fingers, and she stretched herself inside the flesh of the wolf and began to jab the old woman in the kidneys. "Say, stop that!" howled the old woman. "Nobody likes an impudent lunch!"

Just then, punctual as misery, fragrant as the coming of bungled valor, there appeared at the door a huntsman. The huntsman took one look at the bloated wolf, put two and two together (crack huntsman, he), and reckoned all parties worth saving were at this moment being digested. He'd been sent by the young tomato's mother to reclaim the loaf of bread, which she had decided she could not live without. The huntsman, to summon the requisite mettle, lifted to his mouth the wineskin slung over his shoulder and squeezed a stream of port into his gullet. *Drink ye all of it, for this is my blood*, came a gauzy voice, as if from under a hidden pillow. "What's that?" asked the huntsman. A higher-pitched voice said, "My, oh, my, what a big spleen you have!" And another voice, clearer but sporting an incognito hoarseness, said, "The better to chide you with, lovey!" And the woman wrapped in a swaddling of wolf let rip a musical belch, and the girl inside her immediately recognized the melody of those windy gripes, and she added to them by gasping, "Grand-mother!" She hadn't seen her maternal grandmother for many years, not since Nana and her mother angrily parted after an argument about how best to attend to the loaf. The girl remembered the delicious wolf soup her grandmother used to make her and felt a fond stirring in her own kishkas.

And the huntsman, so easily sidetracked when a quarry began to spill its guts, hastily reached a brawny fist into the wolf's maw and extracted . . . a frumpy girl! Whose cheeks were so frightfully abloom he thought she might be better off left to the vagaries of the wolf's intestines, but she held the bread in her hands, so he dropped her onto the ground. Next, with the skill and boredom of a surgeon performing his one-thousandth appendectomy, he carefully plucked a quivering aspic of flesh from the throat of the wolf and decided the old woman, with her long nose and big ears, was likely beyond saving, and he dropped the slop of her onto the floor and wiped the residual goo onto his gambeson, but when thick-nailed, corn-tumored toes poked through the fur as though it were a footed sleeper a size too small, the huntsman reached in again with the resentful finesse of a down-on-his-luck magician who believes he's bound for a destiny far grander than the endless extraction of rabbits from hats, and he neatly skinned what turned out to be . . . a very old woman, ta-da! Well, fancy that. The wolf's weathered exterior, heavily trafficked of late he could see, lay rumpled at the old woman's feet like a discarded cape too threadbare to repair. This nested zoology made the huntsman vertiginous, and he dropped himself onto a chair. Just then the jumble of flesh inched up the bed, enveloped the bones, then slid into the fur and got back under the covers, where he rattled a final breath and went limp with extinction.

The girl, with a face like a rusted skillet, clutched the bread, and when she saw the huntsman, she went, stem to stern, red as the end of the world; the huntsman took one look at the girl and thought *Bolshevik* and decided no brazen-faced rose that rutilant was worth deflowering, bread or no bread, and he pumped the bladder beneath his arm and took another slug of wine; and the naked old crone? She smiled at the pair of them and bowed her head at the wolf, messianic with mange, who had just been alive then inside her. Then alive again, repatriated to the fatherland of his ailing skin. He'd be back, that one, sure as pokeweed.

The old-old woman, much older now than when she'd arrived, a coon's age older than when she'd grudgingly passed down that loaf of bread to her daughter, picked up a sausage between her fingers and pretended to smoke it, then looked at herself in the shiny dowager's hump of a soup spoon and admired the salvaged eyesore she'd become.

The Grift of the Magpie

for TM and O. Henry

It was the day before the Great Festival of Light and Giving, and
Goldie found herself almost entirely without currency, save a few
coins pinched here and there from her weekly parsnip allowance,
and this meant it would be the Great Festival of Light and Bupkis,
for she had no gifts to bestow upon Gimlet to communicate to him
her sizable ardor! What little scratch she'd managed to put by was
barely enough to purchase a pinch of snuff. It was the very shape
and heft of paltry. The thought of this fruitless frugality made her
ears flame as she jingled the coins in her hand, and she threw back
her head and howled like a wounded bandicoot. The universe, as
any liver therein can tell you, cannot preoccupy itself with anything
frivolously bearing a resemblance to justice, lest it end up with little
time left to crank those many laborious gears whose grinding is essential to the maintenance of bald existence. And where would we
be were the planets suddenly to doze on their axes? In flaming darkness and a sizzling winter of capacious inactivity, that's where, so it
bears remembering that life itself, questionable as it may these days
be, is founded on the many infinitesimal imbalances that keep the
day lurching in the right direction. Sad to say, but sadder yet to not!

While dear Goldie, wife of Gimlet, gnaws angrily at that leg of
hers caught in the jagged trap of humble living, let us glance about
the domicile what rings this modesty round. And here we will find

once-sumptuous wallpaper now lolling forward in peeling strips like the tongues of the overly medicated. Indeed everywhere about the room were signs of a once-flush garment worn to threads, a prosperity now decidedly down on its luck and left to cadge the moldy crust of another day. Goldie and Gimlet had once enjoyed a moment, whether begged or borrowed, of relaxed respiration, and then times grew lean as a phantom and their breathing grew labored, and we are deposited on the foot-worn steps of the present indigence of which we speak. Whatever the bank statement might boast of having had, then lost, whenever Gimlet arrived home after an enervating day of being workaday-Gimlet-in-the-weary-world, Goldie threw her arms about his neck and greeted him with the silvery enthusiasm of the moon for the night, for she loved him more than she could love any ermined imperator. Which, you know, is all very good.

Goldie finished sobbing into her duster and looked at the coins in her palm. With this pittance she could only purchase a sorely substandard souvenir of their love for this year's Festival of Light and *Grieving*, thought she with a mournful sniff. And then she poured the coins in her other hand, the hand made of gold, the one that had first caught Gimlet's sharp eye and later caressed that comely cheek of his, and the tinkling sounded like money sprung from a piggy bank. She looked into her hand and saw reflected there her gilded face, shiny and distorted, and she smiled. She dropped the measly lucre into the pocket of her shift.

Perhaps you too came into the world with a body part fashioned of a precious metal that would fetch a high price at market, a foot or an ear, say, made of a rare and glittering resource the world has gouged its own bowels to cough up, a sparkly plunder throats have been slit in pursuit of? Then you know how the cogs in Goldie's mind began to grind. Goldie silently mouthed the words *Merry Festival of Light and Giving, my dear, darling Gimlet*, and she saw in her hand how her cheeks creased and reddened with a thermal fondness as she said this.

Now, there were two possessions to which the Goldie and Gimlet Goldie-Gimlets were very attached. One was Gimlet's beautiful Bakelite eye that sparkled like pyrite and was that winsome green a wan calla lily becomes when kept too long on the life support of water, an heirloom eye passed down to him from his father and grandfather, who had both socketed the eye before him. Gimlet would often blink challengingly at those unseemly Persian cats that looked like dandelions gone to seed and thought so highly of their emerald peepers, and their dissipated languor would deferentially evaporate. The other was Goldie's hand. Had King Midas decided to slum among the rabble and dwell in one of the cold-water flats across the alley, Goldie would have stood at the window and gestured with her hand in suggestive parabolas to catch the sun that filtered between the strung laundry, creating a winking brilliance that would depreciate the king's storied touch.

So now Goldie's hand glinted in the radiance of her sacrificial smile, looking for all the world, had the world been there to witness, like those notorious gates that open onto the Happy After itself, and she stuffed it into the pocket of her duster. She plucked nervously with her less valuable mitt at sprigs of hair that escaped her snood. Had she had tear ducts, her cheeks would have moistened with the momentary regret that precedes irreversible conviction.

She summoned her hat and cape, and they flew to her head and shoulders with a sense of mission they were rarely gripped by, and out the door she floated to seek out at last the Magpie, who had made known to her on many an occasion his bald mercantile designs on her hand. With her hand tucked protectively beneath her cape (thus breaking the law against concealed salvations), she strode toward the corner where the Magpie's shop stood among the storefronts and read the shingle: *Magpie, Dealer in Fine and Shiny Objects*. Crowded in front of the store were failed alchemists in tattered hats passing wands over alembics, as well as ballerinas, baseball players, sharpshooters, conductors, professional sack racers, individuals who had been separated from their priceless avocational extremities and now knew not which body part to favor next. As Goldie entered, she felt her heart start at the jingle of the door's bell and at the sight of the Magpie, who paced behind the counter in his usual contradictory duds, head shining like a starlit night, breast white as the sap of daylight.

Goldie surveyed the store and saw the great mounds of glinting appendages that rose in appreciated accumulation across the store, the smaller pyramid of bronze toes leading to the middling mound of silver forearms, which guided the eye eventually to that grand heap of golden legs, dressed in garters and stockings and high-heeled tap shoes, the strong, sculpted, showy legs of, Goldie presumed, the most gifted Rockettes and cancan danseuses. The desperate amputations of hard times rose in winking mountains around her. The Magpie had clearly come between many a victim of infelicity and her fondest appendage. But there was in the store nary a hand that twinkled in the immodesty of the showcasing incandescence. Gold hands, she well knew, were rare as an albino midnight, and, oh yes, she did plan to profit from this scarcity. The Magpie had a reputation for bilking a golden dolly out of her due by chattering volubly to create confusion and flying away with the winking foot in his bill before she had time to notice or protest. She only discovered her misfortune with the first step of her hobbling walk home, pockets as moth-eaten as when she'd arrived. Goldie knew it was a bold and arresting risk to meet the Magpie on his own turf, look him in his beady oglers as he sat, intoxicated, amidst his spoils.

The Magpie, he couldn't help it, eyed the buttons on her cape, though they were only an appetizer, puny morsel of a temptation, beneath which lay concealed the shinier object of his desire. Goldie moved her hand, the veil of fabric fell away, and she held it resolutely in the air as if bidding on a coveted item up for auction. Do I hear a hundred and twenty, hundr'dtwentyhundtwenty?

The Magpie hopped nonchalantly in front of Goldie, his pocket watch, strung round his neck from a polished fob, trembling on his breast. He stopped, brought his feet together beneath him, and bowed, the eye nearest to Goldie unable to peel itself from the golden glare of Goldie's upraised duke. Just then he raised his wing and fluttered it a bit, a pile of brassy lips fell from a shelf, and Goldie watched the Magpie's beak inch nearer to her fingers, but she did not allow her gaze to be seduced away by the shell-game clamor, and the Magpie could see he had little choice, so he pecked at the register, ka-ching!, loaded his beak with reluctant recompense, and tossed her the supplementary dividends that promised to make this for Goldie the most joyful Festival of Light and Giving ever!

Oh, and then the hours that followed flapped and lolloped in the garden of her heart like winged roses. Do not trouble yourself with malformed metaphors mutilated by a bubbling ardor, because Goldie certainly did not. No, she spent this time rifling through the last-minute shopworn stock that lies hopelessly on ransacked counters every Festival's Eve, droopy and despairing as the day's last ribs of celery left alone on the cart to wither, exiled from both soil and soup pot.

And then she saw it, saw it looking at her, saw it had chosen her as surely as Gimlet himself had, fixed her in the crosshairs of its gaze: a beautiful monocle guaranteed to bring sight to the ornamental eye, thereby making Gimlet no mere prosthetic aesthete. Gimlet sometimes worried, self-reproachfully, as if socking himself in the nose again and again just on principle (from humble and flagellant soil grew Gimlet), that he possessed a vain attachment to his beautiful eye, and when he thought of it, this caused the modest Gimlet to wink for hours on end, making him look as though he possessed the laziest, most shiftless, most leaden of eyelids. But with this monocle, his would be a grand jewel of a peeper that could now read signs and gaze meaningfully and perform all the duties and tasks any smugly sighted eye could carry out. The family eye, as beautiful a bauble as never gandered, would now not only be a ravishing looker but beam with green purpose as well! She plunked her hand money onto the counter and rushed home with the monocle clutched tightly in the orphaned hand that remained.

When Goldie arrived home, she looked at the air at the end of her coat sleeve, thought briefly of all the applauding and cats-cradling and thumb-twiddling she'd no longer be able to do, and decided she must do something to dim that conspicuous absence. She took from the top of their tiny festival shrub the cardboard angel with the pipe-cleaner wings and halo that, whenever it was jostled, snowed gold glitter upon the floor, and she attached it, festively, to the end of her arm. This, dear friends who might likewise be contemplating holiday self-mutilation as a way of financing love, is what those martyred limbs who spend their afterlife in the Magpie's deceptive nest amidst a pile of like-minded parts would want us to do: soldier on, make do with the ever-thinning winter rations of resourcefulness. She choked back a fleeting nostalgia for the play of light that always bedazzled her this time of day, shards caroming sharply from wall to wall, as she sat in the falling light with a steaming mug clutched in her fist, and she thought instead of all the decorative uses to which that absence could now be put. Yes, it was a fine part to lack, the finest, and Gimlet would see this as well, see it with his new monocle! What choice had she anyway? She could not give her dear Gimlet the usual handful of lint for festival, could she? Such a woefully practical gift, at which recipients always nodded with the subdued gratitude such affordable gifts rightly gross.

At 7:00, Goldie had changed into the green gauze of this year's official festival costume, and the pot on the stove bubbled with the evening burgoo. Gimlet was never truant, his heart ever eager to make its way home to the blood it most longed to course with, to the life fluid of his favorite hemogoblin Goldie. Goldie turned the monocle over and over in her widowed hand and then heard Gimlet's key click-clack in the lock. She looked down at the angel at the end of her arm, whose glittery body was quickly balding from the movement, and she said to herself, oh please let Gimlet still admire my tarnished remains, whose high glow was surrendered to the good intentions braised brown by love's blinding flame!

Gimlet came through the door strangely sideways and immediately his sighted eye fell upon the cardboard angel drooping from Goldie's sleeve, and a look she could not decode marched across the features of his face. "Gimlet, my platypus, my ham on rye, my bottle of aspirin! Oh, I had to amputate, I had to, for I could not spend another festival with only a fistful of lint to show for it, practical and affordable as such a present is. I just couldn't! You can love a Goldie without a golden paw, can't you, can't you love a single-handed Goldie as much as a double, oh, can't you, Gimlet, my potable water, my Mix Master, my Romania, my branding iron? Wait till you see what the hand has gained us in its ambidextrous barter." She could not bear to see any disappointment in Gimlet's eyes, flesh or fabricated, and so she did not look into his face.

Gimlet said, "Your hand. You've cut off your hand? The hand I first held?"

"Cut it off and sold it, Gimlet! It was only the collateral of our love!"

"I know your limbs have always grown fast, Goldie, but that one . . . will it . . . will it grow back?"

Goldie shook her head and looked at the angel, now nearly white from unintended, off-label use, which is always hard on an ornament. "I love you more than . . . than . . . five gold fingers can factor," said Goldie, with unusual arithmetic conviction, and then she shuffled to the stove to ladle the burgoo, but Gimlet intervened and he wrapped his arms around her.

Let us here whistle divertingly into the air and cast our gaze in a less intimate direction, let it fall upon some innocuous trifle gathering dust alone in a corner. Be you a rich man or a poor man, what difference does it make in the end? If you were not born in a manger beneath the Star of Go, you will reach the same nadir we all do. Only when you are the most immaculate sort of suckling and attended by shepherds are the Magpies compelled to defy the con in their breasts, to flimflam their own nature, and bring to you a brightly shining future (though one that carries with it a bit of a whopping tariff, kaflerf!). There's a chance that light will be thrown on this willful occlusion soon enough, so keep your trousers hitched.

"Oh, Goldie, my Goldie, the glint in my spurious eye, do not fear diminution of my heart's zeal for you. No, do not trepidate, my rutabaga, my treble clef, my quarter to three. But I must ask you to disrobe that object there, what is swaddled in woolen wrapping and itches to be naked as the bosom of dawn, the backside of dusk."

Goldie took her homely, abandoned hand from beneath the green gauze of her festival frock, and she plucked the string from the package. And there she saw, why, it was a ring, a ring of a hard but linty substance, the suggestive pink of a conch shell's spiraling thigh and smelling vaguely vegetable in origin, and she speared it with her middle finger, but it was, oh!, far too, oh, big! It was, oh-oh!, a ring whose destination was the stout finger of a golden hand! Indeed it was the very finger girdle of wedlock she had so long admired in the lint-smithy's window! The delectable bangle you might receive and relinquish five times were you a pentapopemptic (though this was not her ambition). Yes, it was a ring promised to a hand now gone and not soon to return, prestidigitated away and lost in the occult ether like the rabbit of an absentminded magician.

"You see, when you wear it, it turns the second hand to gold, so the poor unfortunate needn't ever feel unresourceful or burdened by that dastard the short stick ever again. Sometimes I heard your hand a-weeping of an evening, Goldie, my darning needle, my yearling, and it filled me with feelings of regret for my having favored the eye bribe of its mate so vigorously, and here I thought is the perfect solution to this pesky disjunction of pulchritude! Though, maybe, Goldie, my calabash, my Outer Mongolia, my mise-en-scène, my unmentionables, what I should have done was buy a fetching wrap to en-handsome the ugly hand! Why should it have to perfectly twin its beautiful sibling to be admired? I'm always learning things at just the moment when they are of no use to me, Goldie, ever notice that? Craven goose, red sox on malignity!"

Goldie leapt into the air like a kidney in a skillet, and she threw her arms about Gimlet's neck. For Gimlet had not yet gotten to lay his good eye on the spectacle that would make an honest eye of the other. She held it out to him in her forsaken palm, and it attracted that rogue light that used to be sweet on her hand. "Ain't it a dandy, Gimlet? It will give your eye something to light on, a sightless patrilineal trophy no more! Come, let us gate that green god. That is one horse that surely longs for the paddock."

Gimlet, who'd been standing carefully in profile, the left hemisphere of his head concealed from Goldie, grinned a half grin and said, "Oh, Goldie, why don't we put away this evidence of our mutual tenderness, you ladle up the burgoo, and we bask in its viscous beneficence." And then he slowly turned his head so that Goldie could finally see the lonely socket. "Sold it," said Gimlet, "so's I could buy you that ring." Goldie's mouth and eyes rounded in that great triangular triplet of Os that is stunned love as it recognizes in the mirror of its object its identical replication.

The Magpie, as you know, is a feathered finagler, a junkie for bling always on the jones, a grifter of glitz. His aboriginal appetite for light began when he first espied the Star of Go and followed the mythic shine to the light's nativity. *I would give my right wing to possess that light*, thought the Magpie, and for shame for he was in the presence of the Son of Go, who lay peddling his plump legs in the manger (legs the Magpie could not help but think of roasting on a spit). And it is at this moment in history when limbs that caught light began to spring from otherwise dull and dreamless bodies, and the Grift of the Magpie was born, which, to this day, say what you will, bankrolls in its way the heart's commerce, as we've seen. But word to the whys and the wheres and the hows, there are no merchants of love who have reaped greater profits than have Goldie and Gimlet on this festival night, those lovewumps, who both donated their bodies' doubloons so that the other could be certain in the knowledge that on this the Eve of the Festival of Light and Giving, they had both been worthy of sacrifice; each had gifted the other the unsnuffable candle flickering selflessly inside them. They had done so, dear luminous dreamers, for the cause that is love, not lost, only wandered off the path without a compass. But better to love and to be lost than never to have found love in the glad amputation of the body's light. Goldie and Gimlet, wise as the moon is silver. They have grifted the Magpie, who hops from foot to golden foot not his, whose heart lies dull in his breast with the sad, sad soot of cupidity.

APOCALYPSE

The Incinerating Place

Until three months ago, the dim perimeter of the twins' planet extended only as far as the cellar walls, weeping walls always damp to the touch. On that day, an early June afternoon (though *early* and *June* and *afternoon* meant for the twins nearly the same as *late* and *January* and *evening*), a door appeared in a black wall, suddenly (*like a burning bush in a desert!* thought the twins, who found such a notion no more improbable than giraffes or automobiles). This door groaned open, like a mouth a face has kept secret, and their mother (their sister) prodded them through the twisting and fetid vestibule that led them up and out and into . . . scalding light! Light that walloped them in the face and needled their eyeballs. They felt their skin lifting from them like a sheet pulled off a bed, and it was all they could do to keep their bones from fleeing in all directions (there are those moments when the body's parts act like a frightened mob). The twins covered their eyes and bayed when they saw the blinding lamp hanging above them, its shine draped across the arms of those slow wooden creatures they'd seen in picture books but had thought were only a wild invention of their mother's (like wind and starlight and billy goats).

She wrote all the books they read, and she had many names. Everything she wrote about, crenelated castles and magic carrots and meteorites and wounded black bears and bus drivers, were metaphors, she told them, for the ceiling above them, for the radiator that spit little warmth and therefore protected them by keeping them refrigerated (children are as susceptible to spoilage as butter, said their

143

father, and so they sniffed and sniffed the hidden crannies of one another's bodies, fearing rancidity), metaphors for the headaches that pulsed behind their eyes every morning, for their mattress thin as toast. A thick and comfortable mattress and blanket might swallow a little boy as he slept and then he'd be trapped in the gullet of sleep! Boys are indigestible to blankets, of course, but still they must fear them. Better to sleep like a vigilant bird, one eye always peeled, and wake throughout the night. Sometimes the walls stalked them at night, and the boys threw shoes at them because a wall will only encroach when it thinks you're not looking. Their father (their grandfather) had taught the twins well how to survive the many jeopardies on the lurk on this planet.

Metaphors were things that were not real but could become real if you did not properly fear them. It took all the twins' effort to remain properly frightened. They spent half their days on their knees thanking godinheaven for his unsurpassable clemency and the other half thinking preventatively of things they were grateful did not exist. Like trees! One of the twins—they tried to divide the labor of fear between them to increase their efficiency—had always trembled at the sight of pencils, thinking a diabolical pencil might mature in just this way, rising up with its fiendish head of green hair, growing spindly arms and fingers, and then falling on top of them. Yes, *pencil, pencil, pencil,* sang the twin, trying to vaccinate the planet.

And here they were, all around them trees, diseased with scabrous skin and leaves, their gnarled toes twisting toward them, trees dripping fire from their knobby arms! Their mother had pushed them, panting, through the earth's esophagus, and they were coughed out here, in the light, easy prey for a murderous forest, in a dream with no edges, no walls.

It was clear to the twins that the worst had happened: they had stumbled into that Incinerating Place where bad children were taken and cooked to a crisp, a meal for slavering rats, with eyes like polished knives, who, as everyone knew, had an insatiable appetite for boymeat. Rats were not a metaphor.

Their mother had been unable to rise from bed the day before. They had tried to be good, whispering thoughts into their hands that they passed quietly to one another's ears, eating that day only a spoonful of barley in a saucer of tea. The food came to them from godinheaven, whom they could sometimes hear stirring above them. He wore heavy shoes, and he clomped across their ceiling. That's also where their father lived, in the bedroom next to that of godinheaven. They imagined godinheaven's room had its own toilet but their father's did not. They did not have the right kind of skin to survive in the atmosphere of Paradise and would have turned instantly to ash had they tried to enter, though one day they would be ready, skin and all. Their father had weatherized his skin for the harsh climate of Heaven with a salve that made it rumple like old socks, or like the legs of the elephant they'd seen in their book of the imagination's zoo. (Their mother was very clever in the things she dreamt up! They especially loved turtles, who are all fortification and escape, and they so wished those tentative creatures, looking to them like legged walnuts, truly existed and lived in their bathtub, where the twins would feed them sauerkraut and teach them to stand upright and waltz, headless with joy. The twins understood how daily survival could ignite in a body a desire to be all armored torso, limbs cozily retracted for the night.)

Heaven was one of the things they feared most, although sometimes, they couldn't help it, they longed to dissolve and crackle to nothing like schmaltz in a pan, and at these moments both Heaven and the Incinerating Place seemed almost appealing (well, Heaven *would* be an appealing alternative eventually, but you were not allowed to find it so prematurely, or godinheaven would drown you and gore you in his brambly mouth, or capture you in a glue trap and watch as you wrenched your limbs from their sockets), though they never mentioned this to anyone. One day when they were having this thought, their father was there piecing together a jigsaw puzzle of blue-bluer-and-bluest with flat dollops of curdled cream. The twins were no good at puzzles because the pictures were always so fantastical: flamingoes! telephone poles! dirigibles! raindrops! Their father was like their mother in that alien things were not unimaginable to him, and he stared at the twins sternly and pointed to the final piece of the puzzle, but still they could not see where to place it. They were thinking at that moment of turning to liquid and seeping into the floor of their planet, then falling up into the next life, and their father lowered his face in front of theirs and said, *Careful what you wish for, my little schnitzels.* His breath smelled like the sink when it was clotted with hair and peelings, and his eyes glistened black as eels. Since then they were cautious in their thinking and thought only thoughts that remained solid at room temperature.

Their father was taller than the world and had to hunch over when he came to visit them. He told them when he was a boy, there was a man he admired in charge of the universe. This man made sure everyone's shoes were polished to such a high sheen that when you looked down you could see your black boots smiling back at you with your own face, and this man insisted everyone do calisthenics and walk about stiffly, as if they hadn't any knees. *It was orderly,* he said smiling vaguely at the ceiling, *and you always knew what time it was.* The passing of time was very important then and was scrupulously documented, as were the people struck dead by it. In those days, death was something you stood hungrily in line for. The boys sometimes put potatoes end to end and stood behind them and pretended to wait in line. Dead, their father told them, was a metaphor for breakfast. Many people had eaten breakfast when this man ruled the world, though some people believed widespread breakfast was an unsubstantiated rumor. The twins could not imagine how such a great man, who must have been twice as tall as their father, would fit inside their planet. And where had he slept? Perhaps, they thought, he bunked with godinheaven, whose roominheaven was said to be spacious, which was a metaphor for *come on in,* which was a metaphor for a very large mattress, of which they were properly fearful. The rules of Heaven, with its devastating weather, were not entirely clear to them. Their father said that the man's moustache always glistened with saliva like the muzzle of a dog frothing with distemper, and he chuckled. The twins had had a dog for two weeks, their favorite two weeks so far—they tested it, to see if it could breathe under water (it could not) or frighten the walls with its bared teeth (the walls remained unmoved), and when it growled at them once they briefly feared that it was only a metaphor that had snuck into being—and then suddenly one day it slowed its cavorting, stopped chewing on socks, lay down, and their father came to help it graduate limply to Heaven, its skin stiffening and then loosening at the prospect. They wondered if now they ought to pray to doginheaven (but they feared this might result in the reversal of their prophylactic entreaties), and they imagined the great man above barking when it was time to take a bath.

They had a sister (a niece/an aunt), who had left to visit Heaven and never returned. She had furred skin they liked to pet, her face finely wrinkled like that of a rotting peach; long hair, grey and soft like lint; and feet square like crackers. She was both a sister and also everything in the world. They missed the feel of her against their cheeks. She had sometimes been a blanket to them, though they were careful never to get warm.

The twins' skin was the color of milk plasma, dark eyes floating in their watery faces. It looked like if you touched them, your hand would come away wet and sticky, stained. When the world looked at the twins, it could see their livers beating inside them. Their most intimate interiors exposed, like those invisibly scaled fish, like those anatomy models on the desks of doctors. And the world did look. The world was not raised properly and it stared at them. *Good breeding*, their mother had told them, *is everything*.

I did not stare at the twins—I was fishing the mail from my satchel and about to slip it in their neighbors' slot when they appeared—but I did listen to their mewling. They blinked at me, and I looked at the circulars and coupons and telephone bills, the jury summons and bulletins in my hands.

The air was thinner here than the air on their planet, and smelled sweet and warm to the twins, but they did not know how to breathe it, so it filled up their mouths and felt like milk rice, and they began to choke on it. They scratched at their throats, then held out their hands to me. They thought of the lungs of godinheaven filling up with water, but it did not aid them in their respiration. They both tried to think quickly of everything wicked, but they could not shovel the metaphors into their heads fast enough and so could only watch as the Incinerating Place took hideous bright shape before them. A pair of large hands scooped them from the ground like a trowel, and they were lifted into the air and evicted from their planet. They knew they would lose their skin soon, like shucked peas tossed in a pot. One of the twins had always felt tenderhearted toward peas and regretted their destiny, and though the twins were only ever allowed to eat ten peas at a time, he sometimes smuggled a pair of them from his plate, nestled them in his pillow, and secretly sang to them at night. Peas were better company than people supposed, green and uncomplaining. A boy could learn a lot from a pea, if willing.

As the twins rose in the air, the light began to gutter and they fell asleep, strategically.

When they opened their eyes again, they looked into the faces of people they had not known to exist.

The world watched on the news as the wailing boys were carted away, eyes closed, arms outstretched, dormant grubs exhumed and roused to life, grudging as aspic. I admired them for the transparency of their skin and their willful proximity to infants.

And now, as I confided to you in the beginning, it is three months after the twins were sprung from the cellar inside of which they'd spent all nine years of their lives. Their mother, their sister, twenty-four years underground, had recovered from her illness, they were told, and their father was in a jail. Jail, they figured out, was a metaphor for home. They thought godinheaven must also be in jail, though nobody would talk about *that*.

They had been taken from the Incinerating Place to Hospital. Hospital and the Incinerating Place were in the same galaxy. Their mother had told them about galaxies and about silver stars dying above them and sprinkling the ancient lit-up dust of their deaths across the night. Hospital was a much whiter planet than theirs, with more beds and rooms and sounds, and so many inhabitants! They numbered more than every rat they'd ever seen and tallied on the wall (though at first they did not believe anything their eyes told them. Eyes can be such brazen liars). And so many holes in the walls and moving pictures of trees and trucks and light and birds. Every planet in this solar system was afflicted with the same metaphors, thought the twins. Though it was a terrifying place, they had not yet turned to ash.

The smell of Hospital stung their noses and they tried to sneeze themselves free. Their mother had once read them a story about a nurse who saved a little boy from a mysterious illness by squeezing his feet and praying to godinheaven, though godinheaven could not have been *her* neighbor of course. She was only a *fiction*, their mother explained, so godinheaven did not believe in her. *A nurse is a metaphor for mother*, their mother had told them, but here nurses in their stiff hats and squeaking shoes walked the halls briskly (and the sound of their walking made the twins think the nurses bore a grudge against floors), something they hadn't room enough to do on their planet—they had never known what it was to be in a hurry—and here it was mothers who dwelled in stories. Topsy-turvy! Many people on Hospital were ailing, and the twins supposed they had themselves been abducted in order to rescue this planet from its certain extinction, to repopulate it with people who did not lie in bed all day, their flesh pooling around them, and who knew how to properly fear metaphors. It was only a matter of time they believed until the nurses took to bed too. All the people in the beds had once been nurses, they were sure of it. Sometimes the citizens here had translucent veins on the outside of their bodies and flaccid hearts that hung on hooks beside their beds, and you could see their blood was water. No wonder they were dying! A body made of water is a body built to drown, thought the twins (and once you drowned, they weren't sure but they thought you could never breathe oxygen or sing again, which was surely a disadvantage). The boys were relieved to be made of sausage and turnip greens and sometimes-curdled milk. When they were smaller, the size of eggplants, their mother had pushed their heads beneath the water in the bathtub, and they pulled suds into their lungs like godinheaven, who was amphibious their mother had told them, as happy to inhale water as air. The next thing they knew, they were coughing water onto their clammy bodies, and they felt sad to see their mother's face sagging before them rather than the cheerful gills of godinheaven.) They believed the people of Hospital, so sorely in need of Breakfast, would end up with godinheaven soon, and they thought the sound of all these bodies shuffling above them, if they ever got back to their planet below, would cause an unbearable din. They refused to drink more than half a cup of water a day, lest they lose their hearts to the hook. Sometimes they poked their legs with a plastic fork to watch the blood bead reassuringly on their skin. Blood was and was not a metaphor.

They had stopped having headaches of a morning and this terrified them. They slept naked on the floor beneath their beds but could never get cold enough.

Every day men and women appeared and looked at their tongues and held their wrists and shined tiny lanterns in their eyes (so much light on this planet, a constant assault), which made them scream. These people brought them salty meat and boiled potatoes, and the twins chewed it all obediently, then spit it into their socks. The peas they lined up beneath their bed frames. The nurses looked at them crossly, and they feared that the nurses loved them. They liked the nurses better when they were a metaphor, and they could see now the consequences of letting your proper fear close its eyes and doze for even a second. Sometimes the twins hurled belt buckles or shoes at the nurses until they were left only with paper slippers, which they knew would not fend the walls off for long. Survival here would demand of them a new kind of cunning, and they wished their father were here to school them in strategies. Some days their wits simply fled, and this left them feeling like dejected beetles surrendering, after a lifetime of narrow escapes, to the sole of a shoe.

There were those who said the children were as good as feral, raised by a mother (sister) who had herself been raised by a man no more human than a rabid wolf. At this, animal rights groups balked, arguing wolves would never plant their own cubs underground like potatoes. Such a comparison was the result of all those folktales, they said, featuring lavishly fur-strewn women with tiny hands hidden in ermine muffs, the well-to-do gentry sailing giddily across the moon-tinseled tundra in a gadabout sleigh until they were suddenly set upon by a pack of ravenous wolves! This was so much fanciful propaganda, insisted the activists, and they were constantly having to counter it with statistics of the wolves' dwindling numbers and stories of their natural diffidence, this just one more antilupine fairy tale to contend with.

The world is ill prepared to recognize the fermented irrationality that drips from the still of Knowledge. That's what I think.

Once upon a time, in search of the origin of language, a pharaoh gave two infants to a shepherd, with strict instructions that he never speak a word to them. The pharaoh believed that the first words the children uttered, in the absence of communication and polluted influence, would be the aboriginal true language, the mother of the mother tongue of humanity.

Of course: they bleated. (The position of sheep in the world rose for a time above that of sacrifice. Until it was decided that the sounds were actually a little-known dialect of Phrygian, the one true tongue. Fortunately, sheep, unlike people, are wise enough not to get their hopes up.)

The first words the twins spoke to me were *Incinerating! Rotten bastards! Godingodingodinheaven!*

And then they screamed themselves hoarse. They believed loud noises frightened the light, and some days they bellowed with such force the whites of their eyes grew red with hemorrhage.

What people who live far away want to know is how could a town full of people living above ground not know for twenty years that a man held a girl and her babies prisoner in his basement? That a man sired those babies with the captive girl, who is his daughter (as if this were such an unfamiliar tale). If only these people (who only pretend to be callow as lambs) could grant that we all dwell in the deceptive suburbs of evil, if only they could admit how easy it is to be lured into the dark city, where unspeakable things happen with a frequency that suggests, though they are unspeakable, they are not extraordinary. Everyone has huddled in his loins wickedness just waiting to be suckled. Such is the price of knowledge.

It's true that when I brought the mail to their door, I sometimes thought I heard a ghostly thunder rising beneath the buttercups, a throbbing purr, but there's a sound the earth makes before a rain, when burrowing worms are on the move, and I had thought that this was what I heard, though now of course I know different. What I actually heard was the twins fearing things, staving off the end of the world with their deactivating alarm. And who's to say they aren't responsible for holding this rogue planet together while the world wars with itself? I certainly haven't anything better in which to believe.

I was the first person the twins' burnt eyes alighted on when they squinted the world temporarily into wavering view, and I visited them at the hospital and was the only person they'd speak to, so the doctors let me sit with them in a locked playroom, and I suppose they recorded our interactions. They make cameras now the size of a flea's foot.

Their father once told the twins that godinheaven wore a monocle, and he showed them a picture. When they saw me, only the fifth person in existence and their first alien encounter, they knew I must be godinheaven's twin brother, as I wore spectacles and therefore twinned his monocle with twice the vision. They saw in the hospital that there were others whose eyes swam behind thick lenses, but as I was the *first* bespectacled person they'd ever seen, they reasoned that I must be godinheaven's *favorite* sibling and therefore believed I could be trusted not to eat them or drown them or turn them to ash.

I sat on a stubby chair in their room, and they crawled along the walls, a new shoeless strategy for détente. Walls were not without principles and did not like a too-easy target. Whenever the twins stepped into the open room, they fell to the floor and tried to tread the air as if drowning, so I asked for a room that was no larger than 600 square feet, the size of their planet. The ceiling was too far above them, and they eyed it suspiciously, knowing it might drop at any moment, so I pitched a tent inside the room, and they asked me to make them feel cold and then they slept.

When the twins were taken to other rooms, to radiology, say, they shrieked and demanded to know who had stolen the mattress from their new planet and replaced it with a terrible whirring creature that could creep inside your skin and steal the glowing bones from your body! (They'd seen bones before, after extracting them from the dried-out rats that had died from the desert that grew inside them, vanquished by poisoned oats—their father knew well the weaknesses of rodents. The twins glued the bones back together in the shape of the deceased rat as a warning to other rats that he who hunts boymeat will end up thin indeed!) Eventually they came to understand that theirs was not the only room, and that rooms were being forcibly bred and their offspring were scattered across Planet Hospital, but they were in no position to find this a comfort.

Once, before that day when their planet belched them into the hostile light, the twins awoke to find their father holding their faces in his hands (the fingers of which were so gnarled, they appeared to be a chorus line of dancers kicking to the left), and he brushed their cheeks with his bent thumbs and grinned and cooed, and their mother leapt from the dark and bit his arm until it bled, and their father dashed her head against the wall, and the next day when they spoke to her, her eyes looked like tiny tureens of frozen milk, and she heard nothing they said, and they knew their father's touch had stolen their voices. Their mother's face was blue and yellow, and they knocked their foreheads with a ladle so that they would share her color, and the walls and the rats and the mattress and all dastardly things not yet invented by godinheaven would see that the twins belonged to a woman willing to turn blue for them in the middle of the night.

Before she left my father and me, my mother took me into the coat closet and told me I am a descendent of Kaspar Hauser's, a feral boy who appeared one day out of nowhere and was believed to be secretly royal. He repeatedly asked to join the cavalry, but it was an utterance that really meant *show me no harm and I'll tell you a story*. She told me I carried inside me a hereditary purity that no amount of civilization could turn to soot, and she said I should always be wary of those things that might make me knowledgeable. I knew when my mother left it was because she was about to know something she did not want to bear the indelible stain of for the rest of her life. Knowledge is a pitiless huntsman, and to dodge his sights you must be unwavering and wakeful in your commitment to ignorance. Though I have not been completely successful in the maintenance of purity, I have striven to emulate my mother's example. (When my father could not cure me of my truancy, he kept me at home, tethered to the four-poster, and read to me book after book, and though I tried to deafen myself to his education by yodeling in my head a milk-fed libretto of distracting lunacy: *zauberschnuedel kinderquatsch freihundschnitzelbettchen*, my traitorous brain, boxed in by overly sensitive mule ears, those rotten turncoats, sopped it all up when I wasn't looking. Try as you might to banish it, the body, canny saboteur, is forever skulking in the shadows. There can of course be no happiness for me now, only the stalemate of seclusion and silence, only the satisfaction of saving another.) My handsomely benighted mother was so free of knowledge there were days when she could not recall her name, and the fact that she swallowed a few pills too many is undoubtedly owing to her belief that something as round and white as a pill that makes you sleep, and dreamlessly too, could never wish you any harm. I am certain she believed the more she took, the more innocently she'd sleep, free of the inevitable corruption of waking life and memory. And what, after all, could be more incorruptible than death?

Which is why I fell headlong in love with the twins the instant I saw their squinting eyes, occult grins, waxen bodies nearly invisible with innocence. But now I fear all the more for them, making their home in hospital, fear they can only become, amidst the analysts, Knowledge's quarry. Do not misunderstand me to be suggesting that their father-grandfather did them a service in shielding them from the world; his motives were rank as the rotten meat that he is, and his children-grandchildren were born of an unspeakable knowing he forced upon his daughter, now mad with experience. He poisoned his own pestilent blood, leaving his child heavy with child. But the twins were pure as the honeysuckled air of Day One in Eden, and no taint of mere genes could despoil them.

Had I been allowed inside his cell, I would have garroted their gutless father, their grandfather, as he slept, and then removed those camel-backed fingers of his and given them to his-daughter-their-mother, so that she could lay her exsanguinated sorrow on a square of cotton and store it in a box.

You see how the world has broken me, how my innocence has curdled in the absence of a proper custodian.

There are many places to hide in a hospital, and I found one. I sat unmoving on a box of rubber gloves, for which there appeared to be little need after hours, sat as the moon rose in the sky I could not see, then came out when I heard the hospital breathing. It was black outside, and it was in darkness that the twins had the x-ray vision of owls (sight so keen I imagined they'd see when they looked at me a swarm of agitated atoms, angrily buzzing like a beehive knocked to the ground). They could see insects stealthily crawling through dust in corners, things I could not have espied if a light were shined directly on the fleeing speck of their carapaces. In the daytime, the twins could make out the shifting of light but were functionally blind between the hours of 8:00 a.m. and 6:00 p.m. The first time sunlight slithered in through their windows, they thought the Incinerating Place had come for them, and they howled and stabbed at it with a ruler one of the nurse's had given them. On their finite planet, they had been able to know the exact size of everything, and they measured each object every day, so that they could catch the world shrinking. Kitchen table: 88 centimeters; dead rat, nose to tail: 43 centimeters; three peas in a row: 1.9 centimeters; Mother: 1.65 meters; the width of their smiles: blank—they knew better than to record such damning information, to be found by posterity's twins!

The twins sat naked on the floor, their heads tilted together, looking like an inkblot. I dressed them, waited until the nurse on their floor went to the toilet, walked them down the stairs—their first stairwell—which made them fretful and wonder if perhaps they'd really been in Heaven all this time as the only *below* they knew of was the cellar that was their world, their eternally dusky country, Heaven's homely calaboose, but they each clutched an elbow, and I led them out of the hospital and into the endless night, whose perimeter was both reassuringly close and out of arm's reach at once. When they saw their first moon, they tentatively tried to pluck it and wipe its luminous saliva on my cheek, and then with thumb and forefinger, they tried to extinguish its light, which was a metaphor they could not decode. Is it godinheaven's startled mouth? they wondered. They blew on it to see if it would dim or wobble or cool, and I hurried them forward because I could see the ignorance draining from them.

They live now with me, in a subterranean room large enough for them to race recumbent three-wheelers in circles and safely shuttle a fast puck from end to end, tall enough so that they'll never brain themselves against the ceiling, even while capering on the trampoline. There's proper ventilation so that their skin will not blue with bad air, and I sun them under muted, full-spectrum fluorescence and feed them the recommended daily allowance of vitamins. They are slowly befriending the walls and can see that here there are fewer metaphors to fear. They are not yet sure how they feel about this. I may have to dose them with a spoonful of fear now and again, lest they develop a wayward nostalgia. They each have a goldfish and two pairs of sneakers, and they eat greens when I tell them they should. Each day they seem to know less. I will always see to it that they want for nothing (though so has it always been, desire something that requires space in which to burgeon), and will guard against education, which, said my mother to me and her father to her, is the source of all errant longings. I have begun to read books again, prophylactically, as it is my burden to know what they should not—only then can I shelter them from the ravages of wisdom—though I never read the first or final chapters. My mother taught herself not to read, learned how to forget the meanings of written symbols, the word *love* eventually appearing to her like a dragon inching forward, and she'd slay it with a sharp pencil when I slipped words into her hand. *He that increaseth knowledge*, she told me, *increaseth sorrow*, and it's true: the more a body knows, the more it regrets. When the twins are taller, I will tell them about Kaspar Hauser, who died of the out-of-doors and a loss of anonymity, who died of going public, whose knowledge pierced his heart in the end and harvested from it the noise of its final beating, a sound I inherited, a sound that protects me from dreaming as it drums in my ears. Then the twins will bend their small heads to my chest every night and listen to my heart, to make certain I am no one, and no one is just who I aim to be.

The Sorrows

In 1962, the sad children were born. It was the Year of Sorrow. Those children grew up, if they did, to be dejected adults, and all of them, eventually, hung themselves. This did not particularly surprise the other Years as these were the quiet children who looked at everything and everyone with the tentative twitch of snowshoe rabbits amidst a quickly greening habitat; the ones who were hesitant to commit to movement, as though every person and object were a screen door about to snap shut upon them; the adolescents who, in any weather, wore long-sleeved sweaters stretched over chapped hands; the budding adults with ashen half circles under their eyes and the posture of rocking chairs; the reluctant middle aged who sat still deep into the night in sparsely furnished rooms and whom no one ever saw sleep. So the suicides were not startling, no, but still, it was discomfiting to the other Years. Thwarted therapists resentfully called it the Year of the Willful Failure to Thrive.

1961 had been the Year of Guarded Optimism, and those children found it difficult to play with the Sorrows. As the Sorrows began to hang themselves, the Guardeds became ever-more so until only a tiny egg of optimism remained, which they concealed deep in their abdomens and which caused them to hold a hand to their backs and bellies, as if anticipating labor. Sometimes, especially in the presence of the Sorrows, this made them dyspeptic.

When it was clear the path all Sorrows would eventually take, those children born in 1965, the Year of Entrepreneurial Enthusiasm, invested in hemp. However, because the extinctions were scattered over time, hemp did not turn out to be the overnight cash cow the investors had hoped for. Trend analysts had predicted a mass hanging, had predicted the Sorrows would be compelled to snuff the sadness at exactly the same moment, trees and rafters, cross-beams and chandeliers one day suddenly a-swing with bodies, thereby making good on hemp speculators' perspicacious enthusiasm, entrepreneurs happy—on principle—to profit from sorrow. There was a coterie of 1965ers vying for the title of the Ruler of Rope, and dismissing bleeding heart naysayers, those born in 1950, the Year of Accidental Empathy, arguing hemp producers were practically performing a public service for these doomed mopes by stocking easy-to-loop nooses in every convenience store anticipatorily, right next to the Duraflame logs. In any case, rope profits were sluggish and so manufacturers grudgingly found other uses for the crop, and it settled into its niche at last when 1980 rolled around, the Year of Mysterious Colic, providing an alternative vitamin-enriched milk that led to greater digestive quietude than soy. (Many of those colicky babies have gone on to become remorseful seismologists, restitution for the unfortunate effect on plate tectonics of the pervasive rumbling that continues to issue from the irritable guts of the Colics; collective tremors have toppled whole towns, those cost-cutting cities whose buildings did not properly meet the then-new Earthquake Reinforcement Code of 1981, the bones of the indigent and the wrong-place-wrong-timed continuing to emerge from the rubble of the quaking world.)

In 1960, Dr. Rolf Edelmeyer, of the Edelmeyer Fertility Institute in Zurich, developed an ovary-stimulating drug, ÜberEi, and in 1962, a rash of quintuplets were born, making the world wish they'd had the foresight to develop some sort of peacetime Sole Survivor Policy to protect families from suffering the loss of multiple offspring at once, but as everyone knows, the character of the Year does not reveal itself until it is too late to safeguard against its unforeseen consequences.

The Year of Sorrow proved in some ways to be hermetic and tidy, the Sorrows romantically pairing up only with themselves and refusing to reproduce, if they lived to reproductive age, so as to leave behind, besides parents and siblings, only the already-devastated mates to whom nothing more could happen. (There were those late-in-the-cycle pregnant parents who, upon learning of the Year of Sorrow, decided not to carry their Sorrows to term, thereby nipping in the bud future suffering [which some said is what all children are], stymieing that germinal melancholy just as they imagined their Sorrows would have wanted, those stifled-on-the-vine Sorrows becoming the envy of all the sorrowful children who later learned of these early success stories.) They say, be careful, for just when you think things have sunk as low as they can, they plummet ever further—you tempt the bottom of the world to slap you upside the head by thinking such thoughts—but this was one of the curious virtues of the state of the Sorrows: they were born at the nadir and never expected to rise above it, and there is freedom in congenital doom, so they were happy to match themselves with the equally damned. Indeed, had the Sorrows who grew to adulthood and married believed their spouses might never hang themselves, they could never have loved them. Knowing that they would one day meet precisely the same fate, they loved them with a wild-and-consuming devotion no other birth year had ever known or would ever know again. They loved each other the way all tragic stories love an ending, depend on it fiercely, with inflammable ardor. They stood on stormy cliffs together and looked longingly at the rocks below; they walked beneath a stand of hemlock, hand-in-hand, and inhaled together the heady aroma of extinction; they watched one another sleep and saw the death they pantomimed lying just below the skin of their lovers, and they wept with admiration. When the Sorrows kissed, it was said that the earth's crumbling crust turned instantly to diamonds with the compressive force and heat of one bottomless sorrow meeting another.

In 1982, the first Suicide Marriage Chapel opened in El Dorado, Kansas, where, the owner liked to quip, "folks have been both marrying and killing themselves since long before the Sorrows were a come-hither tear in the eyes of their parents." For a reasonable price, you could get hitched, the owner's daughter would grace the ceremony with a rousing rendition of "Always," and the unhappy couple would spend the night in the tastefully appointed Honeymoon Cottage, with a four-poster bed and chifforobe once owned by Florella Brown Adair, mother of that famous wild-eyed abolitionist ("This ain't no fly-by-night, rinky-dink, sequined-suit-Elvis operation," insisted the owner, "no siree bobcat!"). And then after the hearty breakfast, which promised to pay no mind to something as irrelevant to the Sorrows as cholesterol and longevity, you could noose yourself up and leap, in the eternal embrace of your beloved, from the hayloft. These chapels, geographically themed, spread like windblown brushfire, and now there's scarcely a city with a population of more than a thousand that doesn't boast a few, though in these dwindling years of the Sorrows, the chapels have fallen on hard times, every industry based on the needs of a particular Year necessarily meeting at some point with that unsentimental taskmaster obsolescence. Some tried to adapt and roll with the times and offered as part of their packages for the Sorrows cheap funeral services and cemetery plots as well, in anticipation of the complicated needs of those born in the year 2000, the Year of the Resurrectionists, but that has proved to be a pale salvation.

They predict that by the year 2022, the last Sorrow will have swung, and street corners everywhere now thunder with fiery orators declaiming the meaning of the End of Sorrow. Some say the world itself cannot be sustained in the absence of the drive toward extinction; they say it is only the will to death that keeps the rest of us alive and we'll all burst into airy thinness like fallen soap bubbles speared upon blades of grass when the final Sorrow gasps her last. Some say the world will go dark with the absence of sadness. Others say it will be the beginning of the Great Epoch of Rapturous Light, and we'll be so filled with joyful illumination it will take specially designed spectacles to bear it.

One thing no one much likes to talk about—even the Sorrowists, whose dissertations argue we Sorrows are just unimaginative, unreconstructed nihilist wannabes who could resist our year's impulses if only we wanted to—what no one likes to speak of is the appeal that hanging holds: it allows us time to gawk at our own death, to look it in the bluing mug and see its hemorrhaging eyes, to dangle for a second inside our regret and reconsideration and relief, which, for the Sorrows, who have thought of little else our whole lives, is the most delicious imaginable exit.

But I am the one, the only-slightly-less-sorrowful one (though it's margin enough, and there are those who say this makes me the Most Sorrowful of All), she of patient despair, the one who waits for the asphyxiation of the rest of her kindred before she lets go and falls prey to the rope's sireny lure, and this is what I know: that in the absence of my omega dejection, in the extinguishing of the world's final sorrow, that ultimate gloom passing from the darkening muzzle of the earth, the world will shake its head gravely and fall into a jealous slumber, and await, forever await, somnolent and with deep and secretly harbored hope (oh yes, the world will miss missing us when we're gone for good), the bright arrival of that most liberating year: the Year of the Extinction of Every Little Thing.

The Arse End of the World

When Death was born, it was outwardly ambivalent, gelatinous face pursed in indecision, groin smooth and noncommittal. Its mother, chafed by the additional labor, groaned and pinched it gruffly between the legs. The infant belched at the sexing and stretched his limbs to accommodate the extra bulk. His mother began to caution him against assuming an unwieldy shape, whose gaping appetites it would be difficult to satisfy, but the minute she summoned the breath necessary to chasten the little grub, she fell into a dead faint. With the expulsion of the child came the loss of both blood and that energizing sorrow she'd so carefully nursed throughout her inflation.

Death's ashen pallor made people whisper that he'd soon succumb to himself. And then where would the world be? fretted the famished townsfolk. Surely, Death's death would doom the world to becoming a place whose monstrous burgeoning could drive away even the charitable moon, who nightly sloughed light the villagers collected and was known to be even-tempered and tolerant. The stars, timorous as mice, would be the first to turn tail, and in the absence of their buttressing illumination, the moon would not be far behind. And then the night would come to mean something grave and insular: children would tremble inside their bedclothes; dogs would pedal their legs in their dreaming; atoms would shift and elbow one another, causing objects to topple from shelves; grass would bend against the sky's blind gasping; and all of it would go unwitnessed, covered in the extinguishing soot of an unlit night. The villagers shuddered to think of it.

Death's mother, Dolores Whose Heart Beats Only on Mondays, was the one to hatch the idea of birthing Death, when the heartsore starvelings gathered to brood over their collective woes. The town, wanting for solutions, was quick to agree. The valley had once been rich in high-protein mice (dairy mice whose milk could be made into a lovely cheddar), roaming boulders (which left in their wake a trail of mice ready for tenderloining), nourishing land anemones (though the last of those had been harvested generations ago), and an endless supply of the dust of fallen stars, a popular condiment that made even mud and sapling soup delicious and iridescent. But as the human population increased, the food supply had, naturally, scurried in the opposite direction. People had grown so sharp with leanness they had only to hurl themselves against trees to fell them. The thunder that issued from the valley's aching belly made it difficult to think of anything but ways to silence it, and Dolores Whose Heart Beats Only on Mondays told her neighbors the following story:

When I was a wee girl, I fell asleep in the timothy, and there came to me a man so tiny he thrashed and swam to keep up with his trousers, and he was forever in a rhubarb with his suspenders, which liked to choke the peewaddin' out of him when he walked. He took a rest beside me and I roused. He asked me this, "Tell me, dear kidney, have you heard of the End of the World?"

"What were you meaning by 'end'?" I asked him, picturing the place on the other side of the valley where they say the world's arse is to be found, that puckered culvert through which all life was shat into existence. But that weren't what he meant at all.

"The End of the World, my rotten little egg, my skinned knee, my darling slop bucket, is what we'll awake to once Death has had its fill of us." The last phrase he had to repeat, for he had stood for emphasis and then fallen farther into his breeches.

I felt my face lose its resolution, as it was wont to do when encountering alien notions. He explained to me that Death was the creature that would ease the emptiness beginning to swell the lot of us. "It's a clever girl," said the tiny man being bullied by his breeches, "what can knit in her loins a salvation finespun as Death," and he winked at me, his eyes looking like two beetles preparing for flight. He explained further that Death's birth would be heralded by the clamorous belly racket that accompanies the rationing of smaller and smaller cuts of mouse.

"And that's how I know the time has come," said Dolores. That very night she took those things previously unknown to the denizens of the valley, but which lore had informed them of—gunpowder and belladonna and aortic ruptures and fatal negligence and typhoons and rattlesnakes and unrequited love and ill-tempered pathogens and homicidal impulses and warheads and hemlock and senescence and sinkholes and death cap mushrooms and F6 tornadoes and banana peels and steep staircases and toothy machinery and crushing loneliness and radioactivity and a dash of arsenic—and she stuffed it all inside herself with a plunger. When she felt the pestilent pottage begin to bubble against her ribs, she lay down and let it all stew inside her, so that it might reach the proper toxicity. She slept for many months, and her neighbors basted her slumbering susurration with that thin grey broth left in the pot at the end of the day. In this manner was Death steeped.

Death's first week of life was a right messy kettle of fish, assailed as he was by colic and cradle cap and the fiercest rash and breathing so erratic his every inhalation had to be monitored. The tiny man had not informed Dolores how best to nurture Death to maturity, and so she was left only with instincts she'd never had occasion to develop. "For the love of cheese!" she exclaimed to herself as she repeatedly thumped Death back to life. By the end of the week, Dolores Whose Heart Beats Only On Mondays was worn to a nubbin, forced to consider a course of moderate throbbing on Tuesdays as well, despite her ardent belief in the vivifying properties of cardiac frugality, and the townsfolk began to fear that the hunger that howled inside them might never be silenced.

The beleaguered burghers believed the only hope of Death's survival lay in the provision of a strong role model, but they were stumped by the question of who would be the most fitting example, and so they posted handbills far and wide in search of a mortality trainer. Among the applicants were a professional juggler who believed he could pass on to Death useful information about how best to empty a music hall; a mythical tiger of legendary appetite and the ability to enchant imaginary goats from afar; a reclusive subatomic particle that aspired to be even less; the town registrar, whose bureaucratic convolutions had rendered many a resident unconscious; and that inaugural drop of primordial plasma, who believed the congenital melancholia it suffered from might come in handy were Death to somehow stumble into felicity.

Dolores found none of these suitors acceptable, and she began to despair, but then, at the end of the day, there came one final knock at the door. With flaccid enthusiasm, she cracked it open, and before her stood what she immediately knew was a jellyfly, though her eyes had never before alit upon one. Jellyflies were rare indeed, but they had been spotted on occasion arguing with themselves as they drifted along shorelines or clumsily looped about porch lights. They were the antipodal spawn of mayflies and *Turritopsis nutricula*, more commonly known as immortal jellyfish. While a mayfly reveled in the vapor of adulthood only briefly, its superfluous digestive system filled only with air, *Turritopsis* moved to and fro through its life cycle, undulating from polyp to medusa and back again, forever just out of reach of oblivion. The mayfly was dead before the sun sank into the sea, but the immortal jellyfish swam in an infinite loop of being. As reason would dictate, there were those unending jellyfish that longed for a natural expiration, just as there were those mayflies that longed to bobble near the flame for more than their allotted hour, and so it was something of a zoological inevitability that they would one day unite in order to settle their existential grievances. However, no one properly understood the problem their union posed to the space-time continuum, not even the jellyflies themselves, though it was clear that the fabric had been rent, and, therefore, on the subject of a complicated ontology, they could speak to

Death with some authority. While Dolores felt the jellyfly was perhaps not the ideal tutor for Death, she reckoned he was as close as she'd come to a knowledgeable exemplar, and they wed the following Tuesday, just after Dolores's heart had completed its supplemental beating.

Death's childhood, to Dolores's swelling regret, proved even more difficult than might have been expected. Somehow it hadn't occurred to her that raising a child who was formed of the very putty of sorrow would be an afflicting avocation. Meanwhile the town grew thin and quarrelsome waiting for its deliverance. While both Dolores and the jellyfly showed Death the most genuine and abiding affection, Death was, nevertheless, irremediably despondent, for there was no creature who could truly empathize with his singular plight, and what is life without the companionship of a like-minded misery? The jellyfly did his best to school his pupil in paradoxical conundrums, whose contemplation did provide Death with a wintry sort of comfort, but this did not prevent the boy from sucking the blood from his arms during those insomniac fugues that kept his eyes from closing at night. For his night mind could conjure neither terror nor pleasure that seemed an apt repast for an un-nourishable creature such as himself, making sleep an empty and paralytic sort of refreshment.

When Death was eight years old, he went for a walk with his dog, Mutter, so named for the sound he made in his sleep, and they stopped to rest in the ransacked remains of a field of wild rutabagas. Mutter nodded off and began his snoozing incantation, a muffled grumbling that Death recognized as the spotting of a rodent on a distant horizon, a quarry that seemed at first promising but that only became more remote the harder Mutter lolloped in its direction. Death was always solaced by the sound, and he stroked Mutter's silvery muzzle. Dogs, pond wrigglers, mice, rutabagas, mayflies, all manner of other life forms had a gift for joining the Great Majority and therefore did not require a formal escort, and when Death saw the fine veins in Mutter's beautiful ears pinkened by a shaft of sunlight, this fact filled Death with a grateful desolation.

Death poked at the ravened and rotting rutabaga remains as he waited for Mutter to rouse from his nap, and he rose when he heard sputtering footsteps drawing nearer. Death, terrified of human attachments, avoided social intercourse of every stripe, and so he nudged Mutter, who leapt to his feet and bared his teeth, ready to corner any menace, however imaginary.

Both Death and Mutter were startled to see a pair of unpiloted pants staggering in their direction. Mutter began to growl tentatively, uncertain as to the threat posed by a pair of rogue dungarees. He'd seen the back halves of severed snakes writhing their postscripts in the dirt, but never before had he seen a fugitive pair of human legs fleeing its gondolier. As the trousers drew near, they began to stumble on the vegetable carrion, and it was then that Death saw there was a tiny man bobbling inside the disproportionate pantaloons. At one point, the man had to pause in order to unnoose himself from his suspenders, and this caused a zephyr of vituperation to gust in Death's direction. At last the man lurched onto the ground and sat before them, clearly winded from the effort. Mutter looked for a sign from Death as to whether some prophylactic snarling might be in order, and the man gestured for Death to sit, which he did. The man's pants swaddled him in such a way as to make him appear to have parachuted into the field.

"So you, my rotting turnip, are the one who has been conjured to emancipate the living from eternity. Hrrrrmmm."

"Rutabagas."

"Wot wot?"

"They're rutabagas," said Death. One thing the jellyfly had impressed upon Death was the importance of accurate identification. When it came time to persuade Mrs. Amplebrawn to give up the grip on the considerable matter of herself, it would be important not to tap instead Mrs. Butterport, both similarly girthed and sporting purple moles on their second chins. Both women had somehow managed to weather the famine without abdicating an ounce of flesh and were currently the object of scientific inquiry. Mrs. Amplebrawn had a lazy eye that seemed to surveil the world as she spoke, everyone a suspect, and it was this that Death would look for and whose ambulatory gaze he would have to meet when the time came.

"And this cirrhotic liver must be your one disciple. A little matted around the muzzle, but I've seen worse. And who, may I ask, has been instructing you in the ways of the executioner?" The man wrestled angrily with his suspenders, which did seem to Death to harbor injurious intentions toward him.

"The jellyfly has explained to me many things, such as the following: a single mayfly falling makes no sound, whereas a million mayflies meeting their end at the same moment create a muffled din; therefore, a million short-lived nothings become something, an absurd mathematics. I asked if he were meaning to suggest that assassinating en masse lends resonance to an otherwise inaudible death. In response to this, he pulsed in opposing directions and remained, sullenly, in place."

The little man expelled a scornful snort. He scratched his noodle and said, "You're gettin' nowhere fast, kid. You best abandon that dawdling tutelage posthaste. But I know someone what can give you a few pointers. Kith of your ragtag apostle here. The Wolf in the Woods. A lonesome savage, but with right sterling manners nevertheless, gentle as a dead goat." The little man grabbed a stick and gouged a map into the soil. He then asked Death to leave him to his afternoon nap. The man disappeared inside his trousers, and Death and Mutter watched as he tunneled a gopher trail beneath the fabric, then settled in the left knee and began to snore.

It took Death a day of trekking into the woods' penetralia to arrive at the Wolf's isolated cottage. Dolores had warned Death of the feral foundlings that roam the woods, with their long, bent bodies thin as tallow drippings. As he walked, he heard them hiss and nicker and saw their sallow eyes blinking at him between the fronds of the ferns. He hurried into the belly of the woods and arrived just as the last needles of light were withdrawn from the trees.

The Wolf seemed unsurprised to see Death and welcomed him into her home with a gracious sweep of her arm. "Please," she said. She indicated the chair nearest the fireplace. As Death sat in the cushioned cathedra, he felt a flush of heat rise from his feet to his cheeks.

The Wolf sat on a settee across from Death, and on a table between them was a tea service, cream, sugar, two cups, and a steaming pot. The Wolf seemed the sort to be prepared for any unexpected turn a day might take, and she poured Death a cup and nudged it toward him.

"I saw the handbills years ago, when you were born," said the Wolf. She brought her own cup to her lips, and her radiant incisors flashed as she sipped. Death thought at first they might be stainless steel, but he concluded they were just exceptionally well polished and winked in the light of the candle that sat on the sconce just behind her. "I knew one day you'd find me. You're seeking instruction in the art and methodology of predation."

Death looked at his feet, which hung at a lifeless angle, mockingly he thought, and did not reach the floor. No one had ever explicitly described the occupation for which he'd been bred, and hearing the Wolf put it in such bald terms somehow made him feel as though this universe had squared him in its crosshairs. Why, thought Death suddenly, was it up to him to do its dirty work, its skullduggery? He wished he were home stroking Mutter's sleeping withers or losing his pawns and rooks to the jellyfly or even watching Dolores sharpen the scythe, something she'd purchased on a whim.

The Wolf said, "The first thing you must come to accept is that it's not personal. Human beings are a species plagued by sentiment, bewailing their every hangnail. You will give them, finally, a reason to caterwaul, however briefly, so in this way you will perform an essential service." The Wolf spit on her paws and smoothed the hair on her ears. Death, wishing to appear companionable, did the same. The Wolf smiled and sipped her tea, her amber eyes floating above the flowered porcelain.

The Wolf held out her paws and appraised her claws, tweezed a burr from between her toes. "There are many methods of dispatching your target, and mauling may not be the most expedient."

Death thought about the rutabagas, plucked from the ground and rotting. The people of the village seemed to have reconciled themselves so thoroughly to their famine and their perennial wasting that when nourishment did appear, they could do little more than bat the food around halfheartedly. Death wondered if rutabagas harbored aspirations, if an uneaten rutabaga is the very shape and hue of dashed ambition. There were so many things in this world in need of succor. How would he find the time to kill them all?

The Wolf leaned forward and took Death's hands. She looked in one eye and then the other, as though she were an optometrist, and, emitting a weary sigh, sat back. "There's no saving them," said the Wolf. She looked out the front window at the night as it crept across the trees. "There's no saving any of us, dear heart. It will do you no good to drag yourself through this life like a tender gosling that has been imprinted by all the world."

This was the first time anyone had extended to Death an inclusive pronoun (he liked the Wolf and chose to believe the warm and woolen embrace of that "us" wrapped round his shoulders as well), and this invitation made his head feel as though it were an ascending bubble of oxygen, as though it had detached from his neck and were rising toward the water's surface. It was a pleasing sort of vertigo.

As Death stood to go, he saw there was a narrow table against the wall that held a picture of two wolves, an adult with a young pup. There was snow on the ground and the wolves were leaning into a stout wind. The pup was huddled between the legs of its father, in whose eyes Death could detect a bracing against the future as well. The Wolf stood up and moved between Death and the picture. The Wolf opened the door and closed her eyes and suddenly she seemed smaller, her fur ill fitting. Death wondered if the Wolf had hoped for a different outcome.

The years arrived, the years departed, and it came as a surprise to everyone when it was puberty that seemed to lighten the freight of Death's heart. While Death's fellow adolescents spent their days fulminating about the world's monolithic ignorance and devising ways to torment their siblings (clammy amphibians dropped down their shirts, blunt instruments drummed against their objectionable heads), brewing up imaginary potions that would transform all insufferable figures of authority into creatures so profoundly psoriatic they would be left with no energy to enforce their tyranny, Death was suddenly at peace! Adolescence, it seemed, suited Death, and he relaxed inside the hormonal tempest that caused his classmates to chant maledictions in all directions and darkly dream of him.

When Death entered the eleventh grade, something even more bumfuzzling occurred, something for which neither the jellyfly nor Dolores had prepared: Death tumbled headlong in love. Dolores Whose Heart Beats Only on Mondays and Now Sometimes Tuesdays and the jellyfly had just installed a well-lit aquarium, near which Dolores could read of a night about new and hopeful developments in mouse farming (though the first hurdle, a significant one, was coaxing them out of extinction), while the jellyfly swam drunkenly or leapt from the water and flitted in the bewitching glare. This was intimacy sound as any other. One night, while the jellyfly pulsed with life and its absence, and Dolores drew up plans for a mouse hatchery, Death stumbled in the door with the telltale grin stretched across his smittened map. He hugged Dolores and lifted her in the air, and her heart caught on her sternum. "For the love of cheese!" howled Dolores, who, thinking Death might finally have ripened, clutched at her throat. The jellyfly, who was at this moment headed back toward his own callow budding, oozed out of the tank and gave Death a playful sting. The jellyfly remained an adult for only a day, and soon he would again be younger than his son, which meant he had arrived at a moment in his vexed cycling when there was little left to teach the boy about the virtues of nullity versus eternity. Death could not be troubled with any of this at the moment, for the sole spur of his intellect was Nuala.

Nuala possessed the prolonged green grace of a calla lily and moved like a leaf borne by a current, but she had about her the look of something that had been startled awake while in the process of becoming something else, a look of interruption. It made Death think of his own beginning, the story of which Dolores had told him many times, his own irresolution about being a living thing in the world. But it was Nuala's feet for which he had fallen, feet so broad and whopping that crowds parted at her approach lest they meet a podiatric demise. Feet fanned duck-wide at the toes and tapered at the heel. Feet such as these, thought Death, will bear the owner to the most rewarding destiny, paddle her across even the most choppy channel.

Death understood that his birth had been purposeful, that the wellbeing of the bipedals depended upon each member's timely expiration, which was growing more untimely by the minute, that these thinning bodies depended upon him to make good on their gathering invisibility, but Death instinctively knew something human beings had never yet had an opportunity to learn, which is that incontrovertible absence replicates itself inside the hearts of those that persist in being present. He had narcotic methods for easing the gnawing pain of impending annihilation, but he had no such poultice for the injury that is a mortality forestalled, and he hadn't been schooled in the kind of mass cataclysm that would ensure no rotting rutabagas were left behind to mourn their own survival.

While he knew he'd been built for a purpose, he couldn't help but hope somehow he might still be granted an ordinary life. Didn't all creatures have their role to play in this terrestrial theater? Wasn't he, at the end of the day, just another common laborer? Couldn't he give Mr. Moonmiser's heart a stultifying squeeze in the morning and be home in time for afternoon tea? Couldn't he kiss his wife goodnight and then steal off for a midnight fatality? Did the cogs of Death's life really need to crank any differently than those of the average human being?

Despite his training, he found himself developing optimism, and he saw unfolding before him a life of quiet contentment with the beloved. He imagined courtship, marriage, affection evolving into the sort of seasoned mutual devotion that Dolores and the jellyfly enjoyed: evenings spent with each other in quiet contemplation of the planet's revolutions, weekends passed lazing in the delicious light of morning, tracing one another's ripened mouths, before attending to the household's broken objects; perhaps then children, their crusted noses and devastating tenderness, their charming megalomania and broken bones, the necessary but sorrowful estrangement that is their adulthood; and then retirement, vacations spent sunning their beautifully speckled backsides on the mossy rocks of the outer archipelago; and, eventually, many years hence, their shriveling matter as handsomely fed by life as two bodies could ever bear to be: their hearts, well-synchronized now, would nod to one another and simply stop their beating.

And then suddenly there flashed in Death's smarting head a thought that had never before occurred to him, for he had never before had a future nor anything to lose: who was it that would attend to Death's own execution? He could gently ease his hand into the chest of his wife and cradle her organs, prod them toward cessation, but who would be there to lend *him* such mortal support? Could it be that the saving of humans from their eternal thinning had been predicated upon his own lonely perpetuity? Was this the sacrifice the world, Delores, the tiny little man, the Wolf were asking of him? Death's heart felt like a hand pounding pointlessly at a bolted door. He could not imagine having been summoned to a universe as cruel or indifferent as that, and he booted the quandary from his thoughts.

In school, Nuala was quiet and solitary, gliding on the far side of the stream of slimsy classmates that dragged themselves hungrily through the halls. At lunchtime, she sat outside near the pond, gathered her knees against her chest, and watched the water striders propel themselves in circles. Death observed her from behind a tree, and once he saw her snatch at something in the water and ladle it into her mouth. Then she sat on her legs and arranged her skirts about her like a nest, hunkered inside the fabric as if she were preparing to incubate a clutch of eggs. When the bell rang, she rose back up into the body of a starving girl, though Death glimpsed in her now something different. The mouseless nights had not erased her in quite the same way they had the others. There was in Nuala a dark phosphorescence that occasionally pulsed beneath her skin, giving her wasting a look of hard-won wisdom.

Death had always moved through the world ill at ease, a feeling of vague complicity rendering one leg slightly shorter than the other, his spine curving in accommodation, so he walked with a slight limp, and he could not devise a graceful strategy for provoking an encounter with Nuala. He did not know where she lived, though he'd heard it was in the Sagging Bottoms, the place that had gone the longest without mice, a place where people were rumored to have begun gnawing on themselves, so he decided to follow her one day after school, and he kept himself at a camouflaging remove. She strode toward the Bottoms with her head seeming to float above her long neck, hands tucked beneath her arms, and Death tried, unsuccessfully, to mimic her fluid locomotion. Death wasn't sure what he would do when she disappeared inside one of the little houses, and as he considered what his options might be, he realized they were past that part of the village now and headed in a direction he'd never ventured. As they walked, the trees thickened, and he thought of the Wolf's secluded cottage nestled deep in the woods' dark bosom. Death tripped on a fallen branch, and it snapped so loudly Nuala stopped to look behind her. Death lay on the forest floor unmoving, afraid the slightest inhalation might cause the underbrush to crackle. Nuala accelerated her step.

Gingerly Death rose to his feet, picked his way through the duff, and trailed Nuala at a silent creep until she disappeared inside a cave that seemed to spring abruptly from the ground. Though the mouth of the cave was dim, Death's eyes, accustomed to gloom, drank in the darkness, and he saw light stuttering on the walls. He placed his hand on the clammy interior, feeling as though he were in the mouth of a creature on the verge of a swallow. He moved forward through a narrow bend and when he emerged from the tunnel, his eyes squinted against the dazzle: the top of the cave opened to the sky like an eager gullet and in front of him was a vast pool of water a bilious shade of green he'd never seen, the color of something beautifully infirm.

But, wait, into his oscillating focus drifted a great cloud of ghosts shimmering atop the water. This ghostly gauze emitted a rusty squeak, and as he stepped nearer to the mirage, a trumpet-tongued clamor quickened and rose in volume. It was a pool full of swans! Swans were mythical creatures said to spring up from the clover whenever a craven nidget drops his trousers, something nidgets were known to do readily in the presence of girls and crones. The absence of swans in the village had led the community smugly to conclude that they were free of dastards and poltroons (despite considerable evidence to the contrary).

The pool stretched out toward infinitude, the swans rapidly multiplying as he cast his gaze across it: dozens hundreds thousands, the honking racket rattling Death's molars. Finally Death's eyes came to rest on Nuala, standing not far from him, her thinness exaggerated by the brazen plumpness of the billowy birds. Her face looked pleasantly pained, as though she'd just witnessed some villainy whose elegant execution she could not help but admire. Nuala kept her eyes on Death but held out her hand to the swans, a few of whom lengthened like shadows and pecked at her palm. The pitch of their honking changed, and the great bevy of them flapped their wings and rose slightly in the air, stretching their legs, a threat, a protest. Death could not reconcile the swans to his experience, and thought they might be changelings about to return to the insufficient flesh of the ill nourished. Perhaps, thought Death, all the residents of the Bottoms escape to this sea cavern every evening, metamorphic refugees briefly fleeing their bodily debt. It was through the eyes of famine that Death gazed upon this world.

Consequently, it quickly dawned on Death that what he was actually looking at was the potential alleviation of the villagers' suffering, a food supply rich enough to nourish posterity. Death felt the blood pooling in his hands, which grew warm with the prospect of never having to throttle a loved one. He looked at Nuala's face, vivid with an unnerving iridescence, and he concluded that she had chosen not to feed her people, had chosen instead to be the guardian of a myth.

Nuala sank into the nest of her skirts and patted the floor next to her. Death edged his way around the pool, the swans snapping at his feet with their angry black bills, and he sat down beside Nuala. She told him this tale:

On the other side of the sea, there is a village where everyone dies first. They come out of the dead wombs of their dead mothers not breathing, and so they remain. Although everyone is perfectly bereft of life, they are still able to play games, but the games are slow and very dull. In the evening, the dead crawl into their open graves and think about all the irrelevant food that surrounds them.

Because the dead are inactive and given to putrefaction, they begin to bloat. Eventually, they become so uninterested in movement that they only roll out of their graves to see if anything has changed of a morning, and when they see the sunlight angling across the meadow, flowers blooming, dragonflies hovering, the swans preening their satiny feathers, the dead roll back to their graves, brush aside the rot, and try to relish the absence of loss.

As it turns out, however, even the dead are contrary, never satisfied with their lot, and, like wary sharks, they never sleep, so they've time to contemplate the significance of their inanimation.

One of them, a woman who spends her time stifling gastronomic ambitions, gets the idea that if she gathers the right ingredients and simmers them in the cauldron inside her (decay itself providing the necessary heat), she ought to be able to stew in her loins a bit of life, and so that's what she does, she stuffs herself with that sunlight she sees every morning, dew and pollen and rose petals, the wind in the grass, the rainwater that collects on the leaves, the aromatic humus freshly decomposed, and finally it occurs to her that the single most important ingredient in this recipe for Life are those showy, self-satisfied swans that bend their heads into the water and eat their fill in front of the dead, never giving a thought to the wretched plight of having no need of digestion.

So she rolls her moldering body to the lake, where she finds a great assembly of swans, and she begins harvesting the final and essential ingredient. The dead are in exile from life—the sun will not warm them, the rain will not slake their thirst—and so it is no surprise that the swans cannot even apprehend their doom as the dead chef swings the shrieking creatures by their necks and shoves inside her every last bird, their wings thrown wide in terror.

Death looked at the water undulating with swans and tried to picture this dead giantess, and the colossal pot in which she stewed them, tried to hear the trumpeted cacophony that must have issued from between her legs.

Nuala continued:

In addition to food, the other thing the dead have little experience with is love, and with not even a dollop of this to season the goulash, the life the dead woman birthed was of course a bitter and glutinous abomination.

Nuala gestured at the swans, who had begun to whirl on their feet, necks stretched taut, and, like a luminous spring sky that yellows eerily, harbinger of a gathering destruction, the swans transformed inside their tornadic spinning: when their gyrations finally slowed, then stalled, they resembled a misshapen animal trapped in brambles, flesh trying to tear itself free of a razory maw, an abandoned creature animated only by torment.

Death felt his own hot and faltering body begin to bubble toward a slow boil. He reached out a hand toward Nuala, but every ounce of hope evaporated inside him when he saw that she, too, had shifted shape: no longer was she the one person Death thought might be his own remedy; rather she had rounded into the very contour of his calling, a thwarted cadaver rolling longingly toward life, trying to lure it inside her, able only to brew malignancy, doomed to shepherd her own interminable corruption into this festering suspension between that which is powerless to begin and that which is unable to end. He tried to look at Nuala's feet, those spatulate paddles that had seemed to lend her a steadiness, but they vanished beneath the molten flesh that was now beginning to pool, her features dispersing around her.

Death rose and backed out of the cave, the curdled keening of the eidolons seeming to lift his own tentative flesh from his bones.

At home, the jellyfly had sallied back to his genesis, a handsome polyp, and he looked like a tiny star whose explosion had been frozen. Death put his hand to the tank, and the jellyfly billowed its tentacles against the glass.

Dolores Whose Heart Beats Only on Mondays and Tuesdays, and the Occasional Thursday, became lonely during the jellyfly's juvenile retreats, and, given the unlikelihood of ever finding a breeding pair, she'd lost all interest in the mouse hatchery. She had always been more resourceful than most and was good at reading the sky and locating the most nutritious appendages of the fallen stars, so she had not yet dwindled to husk as many others had, but she had grown visibly weary. And she was also filled with dread by the approach of the day when her son would be called upon to sacrifice his incipient ardor in order to remedy the world's suffering. She hadn't realized how attached to Death, and how hopeful about this boy's happiness, she would become. When you're but a green sapling, you stay awake and continue growing late into the night, your heart pounding with the urgency of your righteous enthusiasms, and in this ferment you scheme hasty solutions to the world's ills. You give little thought to the consequences you lack the experience to foresee. So it is with youth, that time of impassioned inexperience.

Death saw that his mother was losing the match as she tried to wrestle a paradox, and he sat beside her and rested his head on her shoulder. She held his cheek and stroked his head as she had done during his every illness and on those nights when the grimmest speculations, which were a necessary part of his apprenticeship, gripped him so gravely his blood pressure plummeted and the air around him began to smell of incineration. He kissed her on the forehead and retired to his room.

Death lay on his bed and looked out the window at the waning moon squatting on its perch. The regularity of the moon's breathing made him think of the jellyfly and also the concertina Mr. Bumblegump used to play at parties, his sparsely toothed, elastic grin expanding and contracting as he played. He thought of Nuala's incurable death and the nostalgic illusion the swans were able to maintain briefly at sunset. Death thought about the life he was about to lead, the affliction that life becomes when unbound. The only tenable future in this universe, thought Death, is no future at all. He did not wish to be the darkly looming end point of all that was and had been and would be, the assassin of portent itself.

He opened his door and looked one last time at Dolores, who sat with her cheek pressed against the aquarium. He wondered if, after its extinguishing, this world, one of many, would float in some alternate space where, though it did not exist, it would be allowed to miss things. He wondered if the interior of this particular universe would be coated with the resin of that sentiment the Wolf said humans were plagued by, caked with a residue of love, the only testament to particles having once colluded to assume the shape of this lost world. The next universe, thought Death, would surely construct itself more cleverly than this one had.

Death sat again on his bed, and he saw gathered beneath his window the tiny little man, now unmolested by his suspenders; the Wolf, whose patchy fur looked recently combed; and Nuala, her bloated decay girded by something resembling resolution. Death looked again at the moon and saw beneath it there were planets heaving themselves from their nests. He stuck his head out the window and opened his mouth, an invitation. The moon was tempted. Death pictured the rutabagas, Mutter, boulders, mice, the arse end of the world where it all began, all the jellyflies pulsing ambivalently, and he placed a hand to his chest, pressed back against the inadequate thumping. Then this self-throttling riddle suddenly lodged in his thinking: *the death of Death*, a double negative. What could he do to bring an end to endings, and the suffering wrought by their absence, without unleashing some fresh sorrow? Death watched as his hands rose in the air, involuntarily, felt his fingers tighten around his throat.

The End

Has your back.

KELLIE WELLS is the author of a previous collection of short fiction, *Compression Scars*, which was the winner of the Flannery O'Connor Award, and two novels, *Skin* and *Fat Girl, Terrestrial*, a finalist for the Paterson Prize in Fiction. Her work has appeared in the *Kenyon Review*, *Ninth Letter*, the *Fairy Tale Review*, and was selected for inclusion in the 2010 *Best American Fantasy*. A congenital Midwesterner, she currently lives in Tuscaloosa, where she is associate professor of English at the University of Alabama.

CPSIA information can be obtained
at www.ICGtesting.com
Printed in the USA
LVOW03s2336210717

542099LV00003B/5/P

9 780268 102265